Hooked!

......on a Little Bit of Everything

A Collection of Short Stories

Christina Gillgren

SALINA BOOKS

About the Author

Christina grew up on the island of Malta. She travelled extensively with her husband Bjorn, living for short periods in Geneva, Stockholm and Iran before finally settling in Western Australia in 1982. Christina obtained a doctorate in social/political science at Murdoch University.

After a successful life and professional career, she decided that enough was enough and it was time to go sailing around the world in 2008.

After 11 years of sailing and travelling, Christina took up the pen again, this time branching out from academic writing into fiction and biography. In 2018, she returned to live in Perth with her husband. They have two children, a son and a daughter, and two grandchildren.

Also by Christina Gillgren:

A Little Bit of MisChief

Hooked!

……on a Little Bit of Everything

Design and Layout by Bjorn Gillgren 2020
Cover photo by Drew Dau on Unsplash 2019
Available in Print and as eBook.
Edition 1.0 - August 2020

SALINA BOOKS
SERIOUSLY GOOD READING
email: salinabooks@gmail.com
Facebook.com/ChristinaGillgrenAuthor

This is mainly a work of fiction. Names. characters, businesses, places, events and incidents are either the products of the author's imagination or used in a fictitious manner. Any resemblance to actual persons, living or dead is purely coincidental. The three stories marked with an asterisk (*) are the exception, as they are anecdotes, based on true stories.

For Johanna and Joanna

"Love yourself for who you are, and trust me,
if you are happy from within
you are the most beautiful person,
and your smile is your best asset."

Lleana D'Cruz

Contents

*Anecdotal story based on true events.

Hooked! ....on a Little Bit of Everything

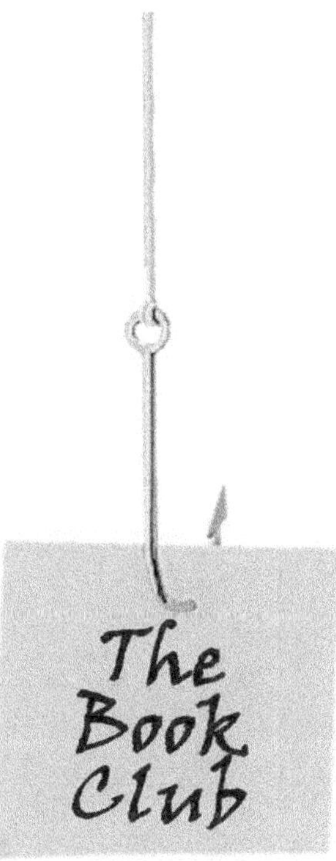

'That's it! I'm out of here.'

Liz drew the curtain in disgust. She had divorced her husband of ten years some fifteen months ago, yet there he was again, stalking her home.

Liz was a journalist with one of the Melbourne dailies. She reported on the dynamic cultural events and cutting-edge performing arts in the city of Melbourne. Much as she loved her job and the ever varying, vibrant cultural life in Australia's second largest city, she felt that she needed a change - and to put distance between her and her domineering ex-husband.

She walked back to her desk at the corner of

the living room. She had been reviewing her options for a couple of weeks and toying with the idea of moving interstate for a change of scene. Her mum, Sharon, lived in Perth, where she had grown up. Sharon had been actively encouraging Liz to move back to the west coast.

The newspaper lay open on the vacant jobs page. An advertisement for a program coordinator with the Festival of Perth practically leapt off the page. She could not believe her luck. She sat down at her computer and pulled up her personal folder. She retrieved her CV file to review and started typing away with gusto. It did not take too long to put together a package with a one-page resume and covering letter. All she now had to do was wait.

Two weeks later, she received a call asking her for an interview - hardly surprising really, as Liz had worked up an excellent reputation among the Melbourne arts and culture community.

'Hello Mum,' Liz started out. 'Guess what? I'm flying to Perth tomorrow for an interview. How about we catch up in the afternoon before I fly back and I can tell you all about it.'

'That's great news! I'll keep my fingers

crossed,' Sharon replied. 'Oh, I hope you get it. It will be so lovely having you close by.'

Less than a week later Liz was offered the job. She immediately went to see her boss.

'Hi Laura,' she started out. 'You must have given me a great reference. The interviewers at the Festival of Perth practically gave me the job on the spot. Thanks! Em ...I have my resignation letter for you. Is four weeks' notice sufficient?'

'Yes. That's great. We will miss you. And if things don't work out well in Perth, be sure to let me know!'

It was a little bit more challenging extricating herself and her five-year-old son from established roots to move to Perth. Luckily, finding rental accommodation in Perth's depressed real estate market was not difficult. She fell in love with a delightful three-bedroom unit in the South Perth area. It was conveniently located a few kilometres from the city centre and the University of Western Australia where the Festival of Perth headquarters lay. With Sharon's help, schooling arrangements for young Tim also proved quite straightforward and Tim was accepted into the local preschool.

<><><>

Six months down the track, Liz could not help but feel elated. She had met some great people. Her job was demanding and exciting at the same time, but job satisfaction far outweighed the stress. Being in Perth, there was the added bonus of having Sharon around.

'It's such fun to be able to just pop in and see you,' Liz told her mum. 'And it's easier to chat in person over a cuppa, rather than on the phone.'

'I love having you around. Tim is such a bundle of joy. He definitely keeps me on my toes.' Sharon answered. She had fully embraced the opportunity of getting closer to her daughter and grandson and helped whenever she could, giving Liz the opportunity to get out and about.

There is nothing like having school age children to get to know people in your local community. Liz would jog to her son's pre-school. Before long, she was chatting away with other mums and a sprinkling of dads who were dropping off, or picking kids up after school. Within a few months, she was on friendly terms with most of the parents in her son's class. Soon, whenever she could squeeze in a break in her hectic routine, Liz was indulging in the occasional cup of coffee with several of the mums.

'Are you settling in well?' asked Vittoria. Her five-year-old daughter Tina was in Tim's preschool class. 'And how is Tim finding pre-school?'

'Tim seems to be quite happy, and he's excited about being at school. He thinks he's a big boy now.' Liz replied. 'And thanks to mum who's been such a great help, settling in has been a breeze. Having a job to come to from Melbourne also made it easier.'

'So what do you do?' asked Sue, a tall handsome woman in her early thirties, with a very direct manner. 'I'm an accountant,' she offered, by way of introduction.

'I've just started with the Festival of Perth as a program coordinator. I'm familiar with the performing arts scene, as I worked in that area in Melbourne. I know so many of the people within the industry, including several from Perth.'

'That's really exciting - what an interesting job!' Vittoria was a slim brunette, slightly on the petite side.

'Do you read a lot?' Vittoria continued.

'Yes I do. I love books. I'll read anything: historical novels, biography, travel, adventure - you name it.'

'Why don't you join our book club? We meet once a month on Wednesday evenings at the café on Labouchere Road.'

'I'd love to!' replied a delighted Liz. 'It will be a good opportunity to get to know more people in our community.'

The book club that Vittoria coordinated proved to be quite an eclectic group. At the first meeting Liz attended, there were two other women apart from Sue and Vittoria; the first was Angela, whose younger son attended the same pre-school as Tim. Carola and her partner Richard had no children. They lived next door to Sue and, being avid readers, they had both joined the book club. The other male member of the club was Paul, Sue's husband. Only one member, Lynne, could not make it. Liz now made up the eighth member of the club.

The evening proved to be both challenging and exciting. The book, selected by Vittoria, was

Italo Calvino's *If on a Winter's Night a Traveller* - a complex book that was both ingenious and funny. It had stimulated much discussion and debate.

'I had such an enjoyable evening last night,' Liz told her mother the next day. 'I was invited to join a book club by some of the parents at Tim's pre-school. There were seven of us, and having two men there added to the different perspectives put forward. What I appreciate is that they seem to vary the type and style of books and include Australian writers as well as international writers. Last night's book was different - to say the least. I truly enjoyed it.'

'You'll have to give me the name and author,' Sharon replied. 'I shall put it down for one of our book club meetings.' Sharon belonged to another book club.

The next month was a hectic one for Liz and it flew by. She hardly had time to get hold of the book and read it in readiness for the next book club meeting.

Liz walked into the café on Labouchere Road, book in hand and looking forward to a stimulating evening. She greeted the other book club participants and then her eyes fell on the one person in the group she had not yet met.

'Hi, you must be Lynne - I'm Liz,' she started out. Then, addressing the group she continued, 'Thanks once again for inviting me to join your group.'

Liz and Lynne shared an immediate mutual attraction. Whilst both were of average height, possible even slightly on the short side, Liz's straight fair hair complemented an alert face with light brown eyes, and her athletic slim figure exuded energy. In contrast, Lynne's more relaxed manner was captured in her mop of curly brown hair and gentle blue-green eyes.

Liz took a seat to Lynne's right as they introduced themselves in turn. As the evening wore on, Liz found herself nodding in agreement to comments made by Lynne.

A natural bond seemed to develop between the two women. The other members of the group recognised this and subconsciously made way for them to sit next to each other whenever possible at the book club gatherings.

Over the course of the year, Liz found herself drawn more and more to Lynne. As they chatted away, Liz discovered that Lynne was married to

Stuart and they had two children, two girls aged six and four. The older girl had started Year One at the same primary school that Tim attended.

'Mum,' Liz started out as she helped her mother prepare an avocado and salmon salad for the evening. 'I've met this lovely woman at the book club. She's about my age.'

'Ah yes,' replied her mother absent-mindedly.

'I feel so drawn to her. I can't quite explain it.'

'Maybe she's on the same wavelength as you. I'm so glad you have settled in so well here. It looks as if you have a lovely circle of friends ...And you seem to have found a best friend too. Not to mention that I love having you and Tim around.'

<><><>

One evening, after book club, Lynne turned to Liz. 'Why don't we catch up for a coffee?' she said.

'I'd like that,' Liz replied. 'How about Friday morning, after dropping the kids off at school? We can meet here.'

'That works for me. See you then.'

Liz found herself really looking forward to the

Friday meeting.

'So tell me more about your work Lynne?'

'As you know, I'm at the City of South Perth. I started out in Marketing, but now I'm more of a community liaison person. It's a varied role as we have a lot of community outreach and activities. Organising the council's cultural events can be quite challenging. It brings me into contact with some fantastic people - and they come from all sorts of cultural backgrounds. Then, there's age and gender and so many other factors. Balancing that out can be tricky! What about you?'

'Actually it's not unlike what you do. I'm a program co-ordinator with the Festival of Perth.'

'Ah yes. I do remember. Yours is an even bigger job. The Festival is a major event in Perth's cultural calendar.'

The women chatted away merrily exchanging notes and finding they had so much in common.

'You were brought up in Perth?' Lynne asked.

'Yes. We lived in Como and I went to South Perth primary. Then dad insisted that I go to Mercedes College. Dad was always out travelling. I didn't see much of him, but he was very insistent about schools. I hated it at first as I had left all my friends behind.'

'You're pulling my leg!' Lynne exclaimed. 'I also went to South Perth primary, and then to Mercedes College. This is weird! I don't remember you at all, so we can't have been in the same class. How old are you, if you don't mind my asking?'

'Thirty-three. And you?'

'Thirty-five.' Lynne mentioned a few girls that were prominent in the school and sure enough, they were soon putting a picture together that placed them two school years apart.

'I moved to Melbourne when I went to University, following my then boyfriend Tony whom I later married. Big mistake!' continued Liz. 'But I enjoyed the Uni years. I did journalism at Monash and found it an excellent course.'

'I took up Communications Studies at Murdoch, here in Perth. I majored in marketing.'

'I can't get over our similarities!' remarked Liz.

The women found that they shared many

interests. As they opened up to each other, Liz spoke of her married life and problems. 'I jumped at the opportunity to move back to Perth. I desperately needed to put distance between my ex and me. And it has been good to return to Perth where I grew up - although I have lost contact with so many of my school friends.'

'Stuart works in the mining sector on a FIFO basis. You know, fly-in, fly-out.' Lynne explained. Sometimes it gets lonely as he is away for two weeks at a time. Then when he is in town, sport is his passion, especially football. He is keen on the Dockers, although they have not been doing so well.' Lynne paused, and looked up at Liz. 'What about your love life, if you don't mind my asking? Met anyone interesting in Perth?'

'I've gone on a couple of dates. Recently I met this lovely guy, Steve. Tomorrow, we're going for an early bite to eat and then to the theatre. We're watching a visiting dance group from France.'

'Oh, that sounds interesting. I love the theatre, but Stuart is not so keen, especially if it is a ballet. Perhaps we can team up and go together some time,' Lynne said.

'I'd love that.'

<><><>

Later that morning, Liz called her mum. 'Can you look after Tim tomorrow evening?' Liz asked her mother.

'Sure. No problem. Where are you off to?'

'There's a dance group in town. I'm going with one of the guys I work with, Steve.'

'So it did not work out with Geoff?' Sharon asked.

'He's a nice enough guy, but not quite my type.'

'That's the third guy you said was not quite your type. Are you giving them a chance? Not all men are like your ex, you know. That man, and men like him, should be shot! Not literally, of course.' Sharon smiled affectionately at her daughter, and then continued, 'I'm so glad he did not succeed in denting your self-confidence.'

Steve turned out to be one of the best dates Liz had. Yet a few weeks later, she told her mum: 'Steve will turn out to be a friend for life. We get on so well, but he's not quite what I'm looking for in a partner.' Then she continued, 'I keep thinking of Lynne. Now there's someone I get on with so well.'

'You do talk about her a lot!' her mother quipped.

'We're different and yet so alike in many ways. And we share similar careers, a love of books and much more. I feel strongly attracted to her. But ...well, she has a partner,' Liz joked.

Sharon gave her a long look. 'Is there something you want to tell me,' she asked, cautiously.

Slowly Liz confided in her mother. 'I feel very drawn to her. I want to spend more time with her.' Then she continued, 'I've been thinking about it a lot recently. Before now, I had never doubted my sexual preferences. But maybe I'm bi-sexual, or at least bi-curious?'

'Bi-what?'

'Oh, bi-curious. It means that I feel attracted to her, and enjoy her company so much.'

'Does she feel the same way about you?'

'We've not touched on the subject, yet I sense that she feels the same way.'

'Well take your time and get to know each

other better.' Sharon paused in thought, then she continued, 'It is not unusual for two people – whether or not they are of the same gender - to feel a strong attraction, but it does not necessarily mean that it is sexual. That's something that only you can work out. Discuss how you feel with her,' her mother advised. Sharon paused again, in reflection, and then added. 'The most important thing is to be true to yourself.'

'You hit the nail on the head, mum. I'm not sure whether it is a deep bonding or a sexual attraction. It is something I have to work out... or perhaps, Lynne and I have to work out.'

Liz and Lynne's friendship continued to flourish, often meeting for a hurried coffee between book club evenings to discuss the latest book under review.

One evening, after a book club gathering, Lynne asked Liz: 'Why don't you come over to my place on Friday? Bring Tim along and he can play with the girls. We'll feed them and then perhaps he can sleep on the couch in the study. It doesn't matter if they tire each other out as the next day is Saturday. ...And later we can open a good bottle of Shiraz and have a bite to eat.'

'Mm... I'd like that,' Liz replied.

Liz was nervous as Friday dawned. She had arranged her workday so that she could join her son after school, and she chose her clothes carefully, unsure of what to expect. That afternoon she picked up her son and drove over to Lynne's house for the first time. 'I wonder if the children will get along,' she mused.

Liz parked outside Lynne's house, unbuckled Tim from his booster seat as he leapt out of the car, locked the car and both made their way through the gate. The girls were giggling away and hiding behind their mother as Liz and Tim approached. Lynne welcomed them into the house, and through to the kitchen.

'I've baked some savoury muffins, zucchini and pumpkin, and perhaps you can help me cut up some fruit. That should keep them going until dinner.'

The kids amused themselves, and the mums chatted away merrily, enjoying a cup of tea. Soon it was time to feed the young ones and prepare them for bed, with bedtime stories all round.

<><><>

'Now how about that glass of wine?' Lynne offered, a little bit later. 'I have a light dinner ready to go. Let's move to the dining room.'

Liz followed her out of the kitchen. The sitting and dining room blended into each other and Liz noticed the photos on the side table and walked up to them.

'This must be Stuart,' she started out, turning to Lynne who was coming through with plates to set the table.

Liz suddenly took a step forward.

'Hang on. Who's this?' Liz queried, picking up another framed photograph of a man in his sixties. 'No, it can't be! Who's this?' she asked Lynne urgently, as she anxiously looked around, unsure of what to think.

Lynne put the plates down and came over to Liz. 'What's the problem, Liz?' she asked gently. 'That's my father. He's now living in the States. He moved there with his new partner about eight years ago.'

'No! ...It can't be! I ...I don't understand!' Liz lost all her colour. She looked Lynne in the eye. 'He looks just like MY dad!' Trembling, she looked at the photo closely again, trying to make sense of the situation. Then she added 'And dad is living in San Francisco with his new wife. That IS my dad!'

'Whaaat? What do you mean? Em.. how can that be? Perhaps our fathers just happen to look alike or ...or they are related in some way. ...Are you sure?'

'I'm positive! Look, he's wearing his favourite sailing captain's cap. He always wears it a bit to one side, in that jaunty manner.' Liz held on to the side table for support. 'Oh my goodness!' she continued, putting her hand to her forehead and shaking her head.

'Come, sit down,' Lynne said, guiding Liz to a chair. Grabbing hold of the bottle, Lynne refreshed their glasses, filling them to the brim with a shaky hand. 'Too many coincidences,' she said, as though to herself. 'Hmm ...my father is a keen sailor too!' she whispered, barely audible.

Liz and Lynne exchanged family notes and what they each knew of their father. A number of similarities of their childhood mirrored those of their schooling experiences. A jigsaw piece in their growing relationship suddenly fell into place. A thousand questions arose for both of them but one thing became immediately clear.

Tears streaming down their faces, the women embraced. ‘Somehow we’re sisters,’ they echoed each other.

‘And someone has a hell of a lot of explaining to do!’ continued Liz furiously. ‘I don’t believe my mother knows or even suspects anything of the sort!’

‘My mum and I are very close. She would definitely have said something,’ Lynne added. Then she giggled shyly, ‘I now understand my strong attraction to you. So I may not be a budding lesbian after all. But, livid as I am, I couldn’t be more delighted to have found you, sis.’

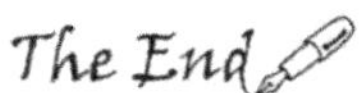

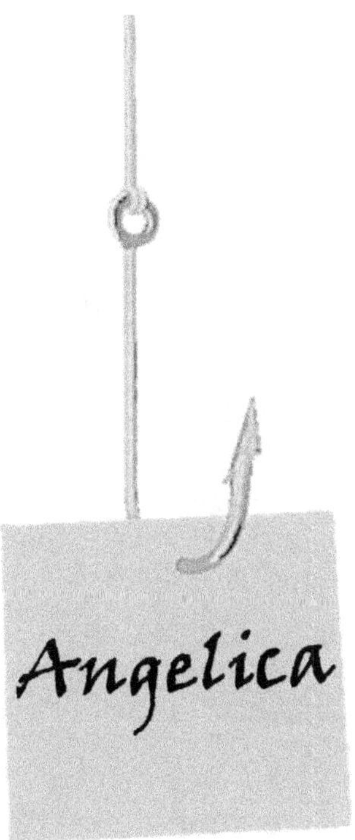
Angelica

She was there to meet Camille as she walked out with her suitcase into the arrivals lounge. Camille had not seen her friend in four years, but Angelica looked as good as ever.

A few months short of her fiftieth birthday, Angelica had the world at her feet. A light brunette, with shoulder-length straight hair, a lovely, animated face and a stunning figure to go with it, she still turned heads. It was not only her looks that attracted attention; Angelica had a personality that lit the world around her.

'Hi gorgeous! Sooo good to see you. How's life?' Letting go of her suitcase, Camille gave her friend a big bear hug.

'Welcome back' Angelica laughed. 'And how's that family of yours? ..All misbehaving appropriately?'

Camille had a lively and adventurous family.

The years had slipped away. Camille and Angelica only met occasionally, perhaps every couple of years or so. However, their friendship was solid, having withstood the test of time. They had grown up together on the sunny island of Malta, exchanging teenage adventures, whispering secrets, and opening their hearts and souls to each other. They had been there for each other: good friends, growing into adulthood.

The girls had eventually gone their different ways - Camille got married, had two children, and moved to the opposite end of the world in Australia, Angelica continued to enjoy her footloose and fancy-free life, gallivanting around the world. Yet whenever they caught up, it was as though time had stood still. Their friendship would resume without interruption.

Outgoing and fun loving as she was, Angelica was very conservative in her personal relationships. It would be unfair to describe Angelica as a 'goodie-two-shoes', yet she definitely considered Camille the 'wild one' in their friendship. Camille had been the one who had dragged her to the nightclubs – that is, when she succeeded - and kept her out all hours of the night, much to the consternation of both their parents.

'I told you we will get into trouble. We should have left when I said so,' Angelica would complain to her friend.

Ever ready with a response, Camille would shrug the grumble away with an impish grin. 'We can't have you living up to your name too much, now, can we? Besides, there are different types of angels!'

The married life was not for Angelica. She worked for an airline company and had access to free worldwide air travel. She could guide you through all the major European capitals and probably around a good part of the globe.

Whenever they caught up, Camille loved nothing more than to listen to Angelica's escapades as she related amusing stories of surprise visits, coincidental meetings and mini adventures. Canada and Australia had been on her travel itineraries at least a couple of times. Angelica could guide you through Rio de Janeiro and San Francisco with ease, considering her frequent visits there. She seemed complete, enjoying a vast array of friends scattered all over the world. Friends dropped in and visited Angelica almost as often as the times she took off on another foreign escapade. It looked like an idyllic life.

Camille often wondered about Angelica's love life, but Angelica had a shy, very private streak to her - in addition to an old school approach in any discussion on love and marriage. No amount of prodding would get her to open up. She was always circumspect about her relationships, to the extent that their circle of friends - Camille included – often took bets on whether Angelica would ever settle down.

'Shall we go to a movie on Tuesday?' Camille would ask, when she was on the island, visiting her family.

'Oh, I've got Pierre and Marie visiting next week,' Angelica would say. Or, 'Klaus is visiting from Dusseldorf...'

Then, just short of her fiftieth birthday – a few months before Camille was due to fly back to

Malta - the airline company Angelica worked for closed shop. The news had been devastating.

Angelica was not at her best that afternoon after picking up Camille at the airport. For the first time in living memory, Camille saw hesitation in her friend's eyes, unsure of what the future would bring. On such a small island, opportunities did not sprout out of thin air. That Angelica had much on her mind was soon apparent on their journey to Camille's newly acquired little beachside apartment in St. Paul's Bay. Gone was her spontaneous bubbly self, though she did try to make the effort.

There were other things on her mind too. Angelica's parents had both passed away, her mother only a year ago. Yet the estate was still in limbo with a host of complex family concerns that seemed to be preying on her mind. It was still very much the trend in Malta for families to rely on investing in property to support themselves in the retirement years: the stock market and bonds or shares were not yet an entrenched part of the culture of the island. Sorting out what to do with tenancies and properties was no easy task in the complicated and antiquated land and tax laws. There was no doubt that liquidity problems were on Angelica's mind.

It was understandable that losing her job – and the lifestyle that went with it – had acted as a catalyst for Angelica's current unsettled state.

'I've put milk, bread and some provisions in the fridge to start you off,' Angelica explained as they took the elevator up to Camille's apartment.

'Oh, a cup of tea will be great after the long hours of travel.' Camille replied. She hesitated briefly, and then plunged in. 'So tell me about your plans?'

'Perhaps this retrenchment came at the right time', Angelica offered, trying to look at the positive side of things. 'There's so much paperwork to unravel, the estate still to be worked out, uncles, aunts, nephews and nieces laying claim different aspects. And that's apart from direct family, all with their wish list of who wants what.'

'Hmm... sorting out estates can be a tricky and sometimes messy affair. And they follow the death of a loved one – so emotions are high all around'

'I can at least start sorting out the boxes of paperwork. I shall move out to our property in Mgarr – far enough from the rest of the family to do my own thing, and yet not too far for us to visit each other.'

'Let me help you - at least with your stuff.' Camille offered.

'Not really necessary,' Angelica replied absent-mindedly. 'And you still have to finish furnishing your apartment before Tom arrives.' Tom was Camille's husband. 'Em... mostly it's my parents' stuff. I have time on my hands now – and only I can decide what to do with it.'

Angelica spent the first week helping Camille settle into the apartment. She was there at every stage, driving Camille around, taking her shopping and offering suggestions as to where to find whatever Camille was after.

'I feel guilty about all the time you are spending with me,' Camille told her friend. 'Particularly when I know how much you have on your hands and on your mind at present.'

'It's always great when we catch up. Especially this time when you are on your own, before Tom gets here. It's good to have you all to myself. When does he arrive?'

'Ah ...Tuesday morning. Why don't you come and join us for dinner – and say hello?'

'Better still, I'll come pick you up and we'll go to the airport to collect him.'

'You're a treasure!' Camille smiled. 'And we will have to start looking for a small car as soon as possible. We can't keep relying on you now that we will be spending a few months or more on the island every year.'

Camille and Angelica caught up on a regular basis. However, Camille was bemused by the fact that every couple of weeks Angelica announced that she had friends 'dropping in' to visit her, usually for a couple of days only. It was like old times. Camille was glad for her friend as it helped perk her up no end.

As the winter months drew closer, so did Angelica's 50th birthday. She had landed another job with a travel agency, which was not surprising given her extensive experience in that area.

'You can now resume your jet-setting

lifestyle,' Camille told her friend when Angelica broke the news.

Camille continued to catch up with her friend regularly, although understandably Angelica was less accessible now she was working again. However, Camille was puzzled by her friend's constant referrals to the 'paperwork' she still had to tackle, whenever she invited her to lunch or dinner on a weekend. Surely, it would not take that long to sort out a couple of boxes.

Just two months short of her birthday, Angelica fell ill with an almighty cold that went to her chest. 'I feel awful,' she told Camille over the phone, spluttering and coughing away. 'I've had to take sick leave and visit the doctor. I've been ordered to bed!'

'I'll be there in a couple of hours,' Camille advised.

'You know where the spare key is - use it. I can't be bothered to get out of bed,' Angelica groaned.

Camille drove over to her friend's house, taking a container of hot soup and a chicken pie she had just baked with her. She knew Angelica was no cook and was probably neglecting herself, especially given her condition.

Camille opened the front door. She was greeted with cardboard boxes strewn all over the floor of her friend's living room, all clearly labelled.

'I didn't realise there were so many boxes,' Camille told her friend, whilst handing over a bowl of steaming hot soup.

Angelica got worse. She was prescribed antibiotics and it was a full week before she started to recover. Camille had visited daily, and was now used to the boxes with their cryptic markings, as she walked past them. One day, whilst waiting for the oven to heat up a dish Camille had brought for her friend, Camille walked over to where the boxes lay. There seemed to be two piles. A cursory look at the formal and neat labels showed that the boxes closest to the staircase contained paperwork that Angelica must have brought over from her parents' house. The scribbling on a second, smaller pile of boxes was in Angelica's handwriting. Camille guessed that this pile contained her friend's belongings – and all the boxes were temptingly open. A quick peek revealed that one box was marked 'births, birthdays etc'.

Camille could not resist. Flicking through the contents it seemed that Angelica had kept every invitation sent to her over the years. Camille was sure that if she dug around long enough she would find her own wedding invitation to her friend.

'Perhaps I can help sort some of this out for Angelica,' Camille mused. She turned her attention to the nearest box and read the scribbling. 'Payslips' was scrawled on the outside in Angelica's large round handwriting.

'Uninteresting,' Camille said aloud. Then she moved on to the next box, which was marked 'invoices'. The two boxes alongside were marked 'for sorting'. Another two boxes stated 'photos'.

'Who keeps this stuff?' Camille asked herself. Then one box in particular caught her eye. It was marked with flags of different nations. There was no scribbling on the outside of this box to give a clue as to its contents. Curiosity got the better of Camille and a quick peek revealed letters tied up in batches. Camille went to the Australian flag. 'Goodness,' she muttered to herself, 'Angelica must have kept all our correspondence before the days of emails - as well as everyone else's!' Yet Camille still managed to rein in her curiosity and left the contents untouched.

One evening, two days later, Camille was busily preparing a meatloaf for Angelica, while her friend dozed upstairs. Camille sat on a kitchen chair to wait for the oven to do its work. As her attention wandered, she again caught sight of the box with flags of different nations. It was too tantalising. Camille could not resist any longer.

As Camille rifled through the headings, it was obvious that the letters were from different individuals from various parts of the world. She remembered when, as young adults, Angelica and she used to reading each other's mail, often over a couple of glasses of wine and accompanied with much giggling and laughter.

These, however, were not at all familiar. Camille opened the first one, with a Swedish postmark...

'*Älskling*' it started....

'Oh goodness! - a love letter?' This was news

to Camille. She quickly put it back, but not before a quick peek over the page to see that it had been signed by someone called Gert, with hugs, kisses and all. 'Strange that,' she mused. Angelica had never mentioned any 'Gert'. In fact, Camille could not recall any Swedish suitors or friends – or acquaintances, for that matter. Then again, Camille had been living at the other end of the world for the past twenty or so years.

Camille turned to another pile, and the handwriting and sender showed that they were all from the same author: Philippe. 'Hmm. now this guy I have met,' Camille thought to herself. Philippe had been part of a group of long-time French friends, going as far back as their teenage years. Camille guessed that the Swedish pile must have been an odd one out. A quick peek at Philippe's letter, however, soon put paid to any thoughts of this having been a platonic friendship.

'*Mon amour.*' ...and not only in one letter, but in several!

'What is going on? I thought I knew my friend well.' Camille almost spoke aloud.

She now went to other piles at random.

'My darling'... this from Istvan in New York... ah hah... so that was the reason for those frequent visits there!

'*Amore*' ...by Francesco, from Roma. These letters had started at least a decade ago. Now Angelica had mentioned meeting Francesco only just recently... In fact, Camille was sure that Angelica was seeing Francesco on a regular basis, with frequent trips to all parts of Italy.

Camille put the letters down. She looked up as she suddenly recalled so many of Angelica's frequent visitors. 'Yes, of course,' she thought aloud. 'Angelica had many friends visiting, and quite a number of them were male.... And yes, we almost always had time to meet the women but the visits were always conveniently too short to arrange for us to get to meet her male friends!'

Camille turned her attention back to the Australian pile. A second batch of letters revealed itself, signed off with love from Greg.

Camille recalled introducing Angelica to her friend and neighbour Greg – and his wife Sue. Whilst cautious not to actually read the letter, it was immediately obvious from the 'darling' that there was more to this than meets the eye.

There was more flagged correspondence in the box. Her lively but maybe not-so-conservative friend obviously had a few, very juicy secrets up her sleeve.

Camille put everything back as she had found it. No wonder Angelica was so reluctant to have any help sorting the paperwork!

'Perhaps Angelica is not so angelic after all. Wouldn't I love to be a fly on her wall when she opens her emails! What wonderful array of 'friends' and correspondence would turn up there?' Camille wondered.

What was she to do with this discovery? For how long had this been going on? How many were still 'active'? There were questions galore.

Camille paused to listen. It was all quiet upstairs. Angelica must still be resting, she thought. She quickly ran over to the oven to make sure she had not burnt the meatloaf.

Camille turned her mind to the present. Angelica's 50th birthday was only seven weeks away. Flashes of her and Angelica watching the motion picture 'Mamma Mia' went through her mind. She remembered how they had enjoyed the vivacious movie, with all those previous lovers turning up unexpectedly. They had laughed about it over a glass or two of wine.

Camille and Angelica had been discussing having a good reunion party for Angelica's 50th .

'I wonder... hmmm ...I wonder. Should I...?' thought Camille, a delighted, mischievous glean in her eyes.

The End

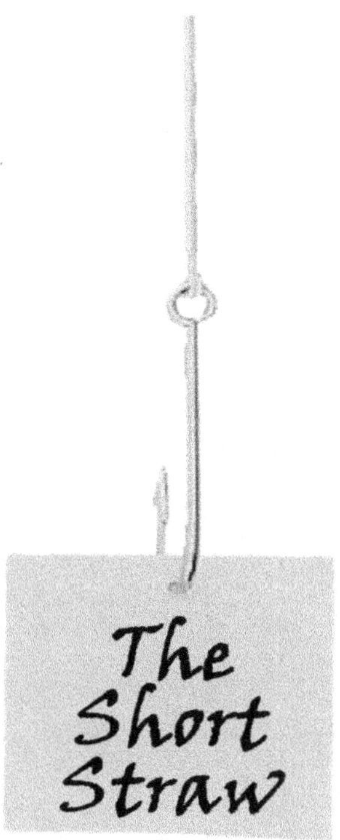
The
Short
Straw

Bruce Stanley made his name as a realtor in the booming Sydney property market in the 1980s and 1990s. With wealth came a fast and hectic life. Bruce loved to live well and entertain lavishly. He overindulged without apology especially when it came to food and drink, ignoring all medical advice.

The property downturn at the turn of the century caught Bruce at a bad time. He had overstretched himself financially by buying into several large properties on the Sydney waterfront. Bruce watched helplessly as the bank foreclosed on his loans, forcing the sale of many of his properties. Debt eroded his once significant portfolio.

Bruce, however, was not one to give up or slow down. He drank heavily as he strove to find a way out of the mess. So it came as no surprise to his family when a massive heart attack claimed his life.

Bruce did not leave his wife and three sons penniless. His eldest son, Martin, known to his mates as Marty, was also a realtor. He had joined his father's firm after graduating in Business Studies at University. Then he had spent five years in the industry learning the ropes, during which time he gained his licence as a real estate agent. Marty took over sorting out the estate. He enrolled the help of Alan, the second brother, who had just graduated as an accountant. Between them, the two older brothers set out to rebuild their father's realty empire.

Pete was the youngest brother, very much his mother's son, caring and gentle in nature. The business world – and the hurly burly of the real estate industry - were not for him. Like his mother, Julie, Pete was drawn to the sciences. His mother had been a biologist, but had stopped working, under pressure from her husband to stay at home and help with entertaining his clients. Pete had gone to nursing school and graduated as a nurse. He was a keen environmentalist and was concerned with climate change and its effects on people's lives.

Peter – Pete to his friends – was in El Salvador, living and working among the Pipil indigenous community, when news of his dad's premature death reached him.

'It's time you came home,' Julie told him. 'You should be here when your father's estate is being sorted out.'

'I'm sure Marty and Alan can handle everything. You know I'd rather leave that to them.'

'Peter, come home.'

'Ok,' Pete said, defeated for now. 'But I'm coming home for you.'

Pete had ample time to reflect on his life and his future on the long return trip to Sydney. He had not quite spoken the truth when he had told his mum he was returning for her. His experience in El Salvador had whetted his appetite for further study – to build on his nursing experience and become a doctor. Part of the reason for his return was to enrol in the University of Sydney's School of Medicine.

'I'm so glad you're back,' Julie told Pete, as she drove him home from the airport. 'Marty and Alan have been busy sorting out Bruce's estate. I'm not happy with how they have gone about this. They would not wait for your return. I'm afraid that you will find they have not been fair about dividing up what's left.'

'Mum, you know I don't care that much about property or wealth. I'm sure they will do the right thing. Anyway, I'm healthy, and I can feed myself. That's what matters to me. What about you? Is there enough left to see you through?'

'Yes. When the banks started foreclosing on us, it was very scary. Your dad was worried, even if he didn't let on. Thank goodness, I have always held my own bank account, and I still have two properties in my name. They provide a modest income. ...And the apartment we moved to after we had to sell our house is great - not too large and still roomy. I love it. I'll be fine.'

A few days later, Pete finally caught up with his brothers. He quickly discovered that his mother's misgivings were well founded.

'The bank's foreclosure meant that much of the properties had to be sold to settle debts,' Marty told his youngest brother. 'A few properties remain which are negatively geared, but their value has decreased significantly. To sell now would mean that we would hardly cover the loans.' Marty watched Pete to gauge his reaction, and then he continued, 'In fact, there's not much in assets that we can deal with now, except for three parcels of land, roughly the same value.'

'Alan and I decided that the way forward with the land was to draw lots. I'm afraid you've drawn the short straw.'

Marty drew his breath in. Then he said, 'We got the two smaller plots of land very close to each other in inner Sydney. You get a larger parcel of land, but it is in an outer suburb.'

'You probably have to wait to realise its potential.' His middle brother Alan continued.

Pete suspected that he had gotten a raw deal. When he returned home, later that day, he approached his mum, glass of wine in hand. 'Mum, let's face it,' he started out. 'We both know that Marty and Alan are – what shall we say – wheeler-dealers?'

'Marty does take after Bruce. Some of your father's dealings were on the iffy side too. Are you going to do anything about it?' Julie asked, sighing.

'Not really... I'll put the land up for sale. It's a fair sized parcel and should fetch a reasonable price.'

'Why sell? Real estate is down about twenty percent and expected to go lower. It's probably better to wait. Do you need the money?'

'I want to go back to Uni and take up medicine. Become a doctor. The Uni fees are quite expensive. Selling the land can help pay for most, if not all, of the fees, even if it means I don't get as good a price in this market.'

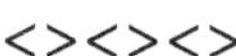

Pete's efforts to sell the land proved to be more difficult than he anticipated. What Marty had failed to tell him was that the parcel of land was on marshy land. No developer wanted to touch it due to environmental issues and cost concerns.

'I don't know how many agents I've approached so far. Developers won't touch it, and the agents say that whilst the land was in a promising area, there are too many problems. It's mostly wetlands. There have been moves to build on the land but a well-organised lobby group is putting up strong opposition. The wetlands are important to the bird life in the area.'

'And your brothers said nothing of this to you?'

'Alan did say to wait, but nothing about the nature of the land. In fairness, one of the local agents said it was a matter of time before the land would realise its potential. If we go to market now, it could take ages to sell ...and then at a very low price.' Pete sighed. The he continued, 'I expected the land not to be as valuable,' he told his mother in disgust, as they sat eating lunch in one of the open-air cafes in downtown Sydney. 'But I didn't expect it to be practically worthless!'

'I was afraid of something like that happening,' Julie sighed. 'What will you do now?'

'Well... Marty said to hold on to the land. Perhaps I can use it as collateral to get a loan from him.'

Julie looked him in the eye. 'I wish I could say that I'll help out by loaning you the university fees, but I can't. I do have a spare bedroom you could use, though - and a study... It will be great having you around.'

It took three weeks before Pete could get to see Marty. When he finally got through to his brother, Pete told him he wanted to discuss financial matters.

'Give me a few days,' Marty told Pete. 'And I'll get back to you.'

Marty immediately called Alan. 'Hi bro,' he told him. 'Pete has just contacted me. He wants a meeting - something about financial matters and that block of land... Do you know anything about it?'

'No,' replied Alan. 'I haven't seen him since our meeting. I wonder if he's found out about the wetlands.'

'Well, there's no going back on the division. That's what he got – and he'll have to make do with it.' Then Marty continued. 'I think you'd better be here for the meeting.'

Marty let a week go by before calling Pete.

The brothers met at Marty's new, plush office in downtown Sydney.

'So, what can I do for you, Pete?' Marty started out.

'I'm enrolling at Sydney Uni to take up medicine. I want to become a doctor,' Pete replied. 'Thing is, the fees are hefty. I tried to sell the parcel of land I inherited to pay my way through uni. The snag is that the land seems to be next to worthless at present. Perhaps if I wait, as you suggested, Alan, the value will increase.'

Marty's body language was anything but encouraging. Alan was no better, shifting uncomfortably in his seat.

Pete soldiered on. 'Well, if one or both of you could loan me the money, using the land as collateral, it would help greatly. I won't need the whole lot, as I only have to pay the fees at the start of each term. I will work and hopefully reduce the amount needed. I would really appreciate your help.'

'Look bro,' Alan started out. 'The banks cleaned dad out. There's not much left and we – Marty and I - are really struggling to make ends meet.'

'Alan's right,' Marty said. 'We're working hard to turn things round. There's no cash to spare. The real estate market is depressed, with no signs of recovery. We'd love to help but our hands are tied.' Marty took a deep breath, then continued. 'Perhaps you can work a while longer and save up before you go back to study. Anyway, you're already a qualified nurse, so why bother with more study and expense!'

Pete looked around the lavish office. He was aware how well his brothers and their families lived. He suspected that their financial situation was anything but dismal. He left the meeting quietly, but he was seething inside. His brothers had taken advantage of him, and now they had rebuffed him.

Pete enrolled in his course in the next semester. Living with his mother helped ease the financial burden. He managed to secure a part-time nursing job working four nights a week in an aged care facility. He also took a job at one of the up-market second-hand car dealerships washing cars for three to four hours most evenings and on the weekends to earn enough money to keep him going.

'You're burning the candle at both ends,' his mother warned.

She was delighted when, at the end of his third year in medical school, Pete approached Julie, giving her a hug and saying, 'Mum, I'm cooking tomorrow night and we have a guest for dinner.'

Julie had noticed her youngest son's upbeat mood. 'I'm so looking forward to meeting her. It is a 'her' isn't it?' she smiled.

'This is Ying,' he said the next evening, introducing a tall, slim woman with gorgeous long black hair and brown almond shaped eyes. Julie appraised the striking woman, taking in the warmth of her smile. 'What a handsome couple!' she thought to herself, seeing Ying alongside her youngest son. Pete cut quite a figure at 180 centimetres, slightly taller than his girlfriend. His blond, unruly locks somehow complemented her smart, straight hair, tucked neatly behind her right ear.

'Ying is two years ahead of me at med school.'

'I'm so pleased to meet you ...and thrilled to see that Pete still gets time to socialise. He works so hard. I sometimes worry he does not have time for anything else.'

Pete soldiered on, working nights and studying days. One year later, he moved out and into an apartment with Ying. Two years later, he broke the news to his mother. 'Ying and I are getting married next month.'

'Oh, I'm so happy for you both,' Julie answered. 'But that doesn't leave much time to organise a wedding. Don't Ying's parents live overseas? Are they coming? Can they get here in time? And what about guests?'

'We're having a small civil wedding. Both of her parents are able to make it. Her mum is flying out from Sweden, where she lives. Her dad is coming over from Singapore. Then we're off to dinner with you and Ying's parents.'

'What about your brothers and their families?'

'I haven't seen much of them since returning to Sydney, and they don't seem keen to keep in touch with me. Ying and I prefer a small celebration with people who genuinely care about us.'

<><><>

Ying was the first to graduate. During her internship years, she was able to help financially with living costs. Then Pete finally graduated as a doctor. Despite all his efforts and endless evenings of washing cars, the eight years of study left him with a hefty student loan.

'There's a position that has opened up in the Northern Territories, working with indigenous communities. The pay is not too flash, but the experience is well worth it. What do you think about a stint in the bush, Ying?'

'Hmm... I want to be in Sydney eventually, and I'd like to specialise in anaesthetics. But a few years in the regions, away from the big cities, could be a good way to start out.'

Julie was not as excited when Pete broke the news. 'I will miss you both,' she said.

As the Sydney market commenced its steep rise in the second decade of the 21st century, Marty and Alan's real estate investments finally started to pay dividends. Apartment blocks were cropping up all over the city, and the brothers joined the rush.

'This is the time to make use of our sites,'

Marty told Alan. 'We can build two high-rises and make a fortune. The market is going up by the day, and the sooner we get in, the better.'

'Our asset base is growing,' Alan cautioned his brother. 'But we don't have much liquidity.'

'The shopping centre we bought into is doing well, as are the other properties we have acquired,' Marty explained. He was the more bullish of the two brothers. 'And they are more than paying their way. In fact, we need to expand to ensure we are able to continue to capitalise on negative gearing.'

The Sydney property market continued its rapid and significant growth with prices going up almost daily. The brothers gleefully saw their financial position strengthen. This was despite the hefty loans they took out to cover the building of the apartment blocks on their sites.

'With prices going up at the rate they are, we will make a mint,' Marty gloated. 'It's always been my dream to regain our dad's reputation as one of the leading realtors in Sydney.'

'Perhaps we should buy the property next door and expand our office,' Alan said. He was enjoying their newfound wealth and status –

Hooked! ....on a Little Bit of Everything and the life that went with it.

Meanwhile, Ying and Peter had settled in well in the north-eastern part of the Territory. They enjoyed working together at the local medical centre. The local community had embraced and welcomed them warmly, even more so after the arrival of their first child, a daughter.

'Apart from the humidity in the wet season, life is quite pleasant here,' Ying started out. 'The last five years have been wonderful – but I would like to go back to Sydney.'

'Ah yes?' Peter looked lovingly at his wife and partner.

Ying smiled. 'I'm pregnant!'

'What? ...Really? ...That's terrific!' Pete grabbed his wife in a bear hug, lifted her off her feet, and whirled her around. His face lit up.

'Guess it's too early to tell our parents, but I know mum is going to be thrilled.'

<><><>

Pete's mother called a few days later. 'I just wanted to let you know that I will be going into hospital next month. Nothing serious...' Julie added quickly. 'My right knee has been really painful and it's time for a knee replacement.'

'Why didn't you tell me you had knee problems?'

'Oh, it wasn't bad until I fell about two weeks ago.'

'You had a fall? Mum, you should have called.'

'Oh, you have your wife and your life now. I can't keep turning to you for minor issues. And you know David, our family doctor. He's been taking good care of me.'

'Oh mum! Well, are Marty or Alan helping out?'

'I did phone Alan's wife, Anne, but she wasn't very ...eh.. what shall I say ...not warm at all. She said Alan was too busy at the moment – and that unless there's something urgent...'

'Oh bloody hell!' Peter replied in exasperation. 'Well, I'll give David a call and get an update. And I'll check on your progress.'

A few months later, Julie had had a successful knee replacement and was recovering well. Pete decided it was time to break the news about Ying's pregnancy.

'Hi Mum,' he said. 'You'd better sit down! Double good news.'

'Yes?' answered an excited Julie.

'First of all, Ying is pregnant again, she's now four months, and all is going well. We're looking forward to a brother or sister for Maddy.' Maddy was their three-year-old bundle of energy.

'That's terrific news,' Julie replied. 'I'm so happy for both of you. How's Ying? Is she well?'

'Oh yes. Not much morning sickness and she looks so healthy.' Then he continued, 'And mum, you're also going to get to see Maddy and the newcomer more often.' Pete knew that Julie was disappointed that her two elder sons hardly visited. She often complained that they rarely invited her over to visit and to enjoy the grandchildren.

'We have just about sold our home, and we're moving back to Sydney in two months.'

'That's terrific news,' Julie said, tears streaming down her face. 'I have missed you both so much. And now there will soon be another little one!'

<><><>

The saying goes that what goes up, must come

down. And so it was with the real estate market on the eastern seaboard of Australia. Property prices reached record prices. It did not take a genius to work out that this could not last.

Everyone held their breath as the downward slide started. The unfettered development of thousands of apartments that suddenly came on to the market meant that as property prices dropped, apartment prices fell through the floor.

'Marty,' a panicked Alan started out. 'Our high-rises are nearing completion, but the prices have now come down about twenty percent. We've only sold a third of them. With the cost blow-outs, especially as you insisted we go for luxury apartments, I don't think we can even cover costs!'

'Hmm... don't panic yet bro. Foreign investment in property is still going strong. It may yet pay dividends that we went for the top end of the market.'

A month later, the news was plastered across the financial papers: the oversupply of apartments had seen prices fall a further ten percent.

'We're ruined!' groaned Alan. 'There's no way

we can recover from this.'

It took a further six months before Alan's prediction came true and the brothers became bankrupt.

Three months before their second child was due, Pete and Ying moved back to Sydney. They found a pleasant little three-bedroom cottage with a small garden in one of the outer suburbs. Pete approached the local medical centre and was delighted to secure a position.

The arrival of their second child – a sister for Maddy – was another milestone for Ying and Pete. Julie came to visit for a few weeks, further cementing the good relationship that she and Ying enjoyed.

'I'm so happy that you now live closer.' Julie told her son and his wife. 'And I love being able to spend time with Maddy, and with her little baby sister.'

'Marty and Alan are fools,' Pete said. 'They and their families could have benefitted from having you around. Their loss! By the way, how are they getting on? I haven't heard anything from them for ages.'

'Well, I haven't heard much either. But I did hear that they moved from their offices. It seems they are not doing so well.'

Ying took a year out from work before joining Pete at the medical centre. With Pete's hefty loan and a home mortgage hanging over them, Ying had decided to work for a few years and save up before she would go back to medical school and study to become an anaesthetist.

Life had settled into a comfortable routine when unexpectedly Pete received a call from a real estate agent.

'Good morning! I'm Frank Underwood and I'm from Star Realty. It's taken quite a while to track you down.'

'Good morning!' replied Pete. He had just stepped into the medical centre in time for his morning patients. 'What is this about?'

'I would like to chat to you about the parcel of land you own. Can we meet for a coffee sometime this week?'

'I had almost forgotten about that land. It's wetlands – not really of much use to anyone.'

'Well I have a very interested buyer.'

'What? For that piece of land? Do they know what it is?'

'Oh yes they do! Please can we meet? Then I can explain it all to you.'

Pete got his phone out and checked his diary. 'I'm free on Thursday afternoon.'

Pete caught up with his wife over lunch. 'Guess what? I got a call from a realtor this morning. He wants to chat about that parcel of land I inherited.'

'Really? I thought it was a nature reserve.'

'Wetlands. At first, I thought it was a real estate agent chasing another listing. But he says he has a buyer. I'm curious to see what he has to say.'

Pete arrived at the appointed time for the meeting.

'Good afternoon, Peter. Frank Underwood,' the realtor introduced himself. 'Thanks for making the time to meet with me.'

'Hello Frank,' Pete replied. 'So what's this all about?'

Frank ordered two coffees and pulled out a pile of papers from his folder. 'I have been approached by the director of one of the major shopping mall chains. These people are very well established and well regarded in the industry. They are interested in the parcel of land you own. I have a serious offer to put to you on their behalf.'

'What? ...I have had that land for some time – almost two decades. I tried to sell it, but nobody would touch it, especially developers. Its wetlands and it seems that there is opposition to any development. If your clients are serious, they would know this. So what has changed?'

'Ah!' Frank stated. 'A lot has changed. In fact, a couple of things have come together. Housing has gone up surrounding what was once the wetlands.'

'What do you mean? What happened to the wetlands?'

'Climate change coupled with housing density have transformed marshy land into an arid waste. The parcel of land is large, but not enough for the wetlands ecosystem to survive. In fact, they have practically dried up. The land is now more of an eyesore. The residents are lobbying to do something about it as some dumping of rubbish takes place.'

'That's an incredible turn around.'

'Yes, indeed!' Frank went on. 'And it gets better. The land is ideally situated, surrounded by a rapidly growing community. So the developers want to build a large shopping mall and include some community facilities.'

Frank referred to his sheaf of papers and selected what looked like an offer of sale and purchase. 'My clients are willing to offer you six million dollars for the land. It is a fair offer, given that there will still be some remedial work to do to ensure that heavy rains will not turn it into a temporary swamp.'

'Goodness!' Pete looked on in disbelief. 'I have to think about this.'

'Here's my card. Can you get back to me by the end of next week?'

Pete could not wait to get home to tell Ying the news.

'It's almost too good to be true,' Pete started out. 'But before we get carried away, I must make sure that it is no longer viable wetlands.'

It took Pete a full week to gather the information he required. With the status of the wetlands verified, Peter was ready to move on.

'Looks like we're all set to go ahead and accept the offer,' Pete told Ying. 'Six million dollars! It's bizarre.'

'I still can't believe it's happening!' his wife replied.

'I thought that I had really drawn the short straw when my brothers divided up dad's estate: a worthless piece of land. Well it has finally paid off – more than I ever imagined possible. I can now repay my student loan. And you can start on your studies immediately - if you're still keen on becoming an anaesthetist, that is.'

'Of course! I love what I do, and anaesthetics interest me greatly. What about you?'

'I've been toying with an idea. What say we negotiate with the shopping mall developers to include a large medical and community centre? We can offer low cost medical services. And do you remember that Swedish experiment with housing for seniors? Perhaps we can tempt them to include some accommodation on top of the mall for seniors, people with disabilities and others who can live independently. Can you imagine the benefits of being able to take an elevator down for a cup of coffee, a library, and some shopping thrown in?'

'Ha! You're still the idealist I met so many years ago. But that's a great idea. Let's see if they see it the same way.'

Pete met with the realtor and the developers to accept the offer. The inclusion of a medical and community centre was easy to achieve. In addition, the developers promised to explore further Pete's suggestions of including special housing on top of the mall. However, Pete was not holding his breath over this.

With the windfall deposited into his bank account, Pete and Ying turned their attention to their needs once more.

'I think it is also time to move. The girls are growing and it's good to have a spare bedroom for when your mum and one of my parents visit,' Ying said.

'Good!' Pete replied. 'That's another thing I have been dreaming of – building a zero energy home that doesn't require cooling and heating and uses very little energy for the rest of our needs.'

Then he looked at Ying shyly. "There is one indulgence I would like.'

'And what's that,' laughed Ying.

'A Tesla. I spotted a year-old SUV on the internet the other day. It's at the Sydney car yard where I used to wash cars. Do you remember that? It's not far from here.'

'An electric car? Why am I not surprised? But a Tesla? Very upmarket! Not your usual style,' Ying teased, nudging her husband affectionately. 'Let's go and get it then - tomorrow! You might even be remembered by some of the people who work there.'

Pete and Ying drove to the car yard the next day, as planned. They were busily examining the car. Then, out of the corner of his eye, Pete caught sight of a salesperson wearing the yard's iconic light blue jacket. As he approached, Pete turned to greet him. He could not have been more surprised.

'Marty?' he said, as recognition - and disbelief dawned. 'What are YOU doing here?'

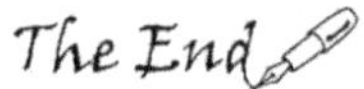

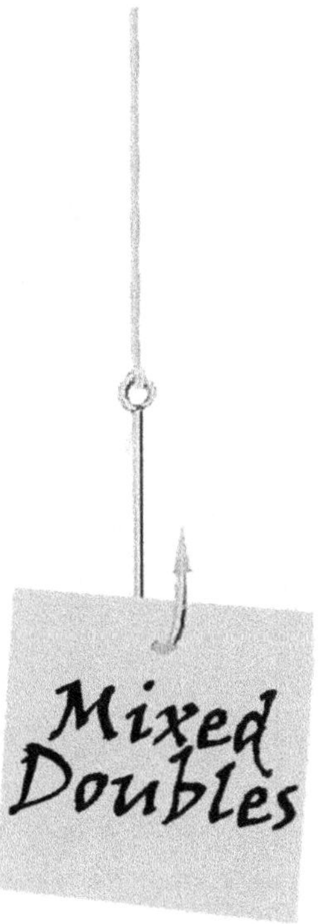
Mixed
Doubles

The one constant in Helen's busy life was the Thursday card game.

Helen, a lawyer specialising in real estate property settlement, worked and lived in the leafy beach suburb of Cottesloe. She was a stunning looker, auburn short hair and hazel eyes that twinkled with merriment as she waltzed through life with a perennial smile on her face. Her regular gym visits kept her in excellent shape so that, whilst in her late forties, she still kept men's heads turning. She was always on the go, driving around in her black Saab Aero convertible.

Helen was an avid patron of the arts. She only

seemed to catch up with her husband Michael in the evenings, as they both were regular theatregoers. In addition, she somehow managed to squeeze in a passion for tennis to complement her love of cards.

Helen's closest friend and fellow card player was Carol, who lived just around the corner from her.

Carol and Helen walked together along Cottesloe beach early every morning, as immaculately turned out in their sports clothes as in everything else they wore. Yet, they could not have been more different. Carol was a yoga instructor, who exuded a calmness that belied her sharp mind. This made her a worthy and challenging opponent in the weekly rummy game. She wore her short, blond hair tied back in the fashionable Claremont bob and was attractive but somewhat shy. Five years Helen's junior and at almost 1.8 metres, she dwarfed Helen when she walked beside her. She stooped slightly as she listened attentively to her friend's chatter. Carol shared Helen's passion for tennis. They had travelled to Wimbledon the previous year to watch the tennis tournament in which their beloved Roger Federer had carried the men's title.

Carol had come into Helen's life twenty years previously when she had married Helen's husband's younger brother, Patrick. Michael and Patrick had inherited their father's well-established jewellery enterprise but unfortunately, the brothers had fallen out over a decade ago. Now they were business competitors and rivals. Despite this, the girls enjoyed an enduring friendship.

The other members of the informal rummy club were Maggie and Sharon. Maggie was a live wire, bubbly and gregarious, and with a wicked sense of humour. She kept the group in stitches with her antics. A wealthy divorcee, she flitted between partners depending on her moods, flying around the world and mixing with the Perth high-fliers. She loved wearing red lipstick and red stilettos which not only contrasted with her raven black hair but also added to her 1.7 metres. Her arrival was often preceded by the sound of the distinct clicking of her heels on floors.

Sharon was a different cup of tea altogether. She and husband Mel ran a successful bookshop cum café in trendy Claremont. Approximately the same height as Maggie, she differed in every other aspect. With light brown soft curly hair and a more rotund build, Sharon had a homely, comforting appearance that belied a impish sense of humour. She was closer to Maggie, and they often went to the theatre - which Mel hated - together. She was a little bit in awe of Maggie's larger-than-life character, and certainly could not compete with the eclectic lifestyle.

Finally, there was Camille.

A fifth member of the card club had pulled out two years ago, when she had moved away from Perth to Sydney. It was then that Helen had invited Camille to join the group. Helen had done the settlement for Camille's new property in Perth and the women had hit it off immediately. Camille was a freelance journalist specialising in lifestyle issues. Her short mop of hair framed an alert face and added to the energy that seemed to exude from her. Camille and Helen had taken to meeting for coffee a couple of times a week, after a robust session at the gym they both attended.

The card group had been playing cards together for over twenty years, spending many pleasant afternoons at the coffee shop by the sea in Port Beach, which provided an excellent ambience. They met at 4.00pm on Thursdays and played late into the evening, usually sharing a few platters washed down by - of course - the best of Western Australian wine.

The group welcomed Camille into their fold. Camille got to like and appreciate this lively and entertaining group of women. She enjoyed the friendly banter and camaraderie of the group, and it was not long before she was also part of their social circle.

Mischievous Maggie kept the group well entertained with the latest gossip, or news of her own exploits, often egged on and supported by Sharon. It was better than the best TV soap. And who better to tell than the effervescent Maggie.

Helen and, less so, Carol joined in the banter, with the occasional foray into naughty jokes and ribald comment. The only time Carol truly came alive was when she spoke of her two loves: yoga, and tennis, waxing lyrical about Federer or as she regaled Muguruza's commanding performance at the women's final match at Wimbledon where she defeated Venus Williams.

Conversation ebbed and flowed, as the group played round after round of rummy. They played on a points system, and the day's overall winner would be the recipient of a good bottle of wine to which they had all contributed.

The card games were a welcome break from the weekly work routine. Many of the regulars at the beach club came to know the women. Of course, there was also the local gigolo who had a crush on Carol. Week after week, he would turn up, gushing complements, trying to break into their circle by offering a round of drinks. The group watched his futile efforts in amusements. These included donning and parading a series of budgie smugglers, the most obscene of which were white!

'Here he comes, Carol. ...Wearing yellow today. Do you think he pads it up with nylons?' Helen teased, a naughty grin so broad it almost split her face.

'I like the bathers with the eagle on the front,' Maggie added naughtily. 'What does he say when he 'scores'? "The eagle had landed?"'

Through bursts of laughter, Carol turned crimson but managed a wry smile. 'I wish he'd focus his attention on one of you lot instead!'

Camille could not miss the occasional

surreptitious look that passed between Helen and Carol, even though the rest seemed oblivious. She had noticed this exchange on a number of occasions and thought nothing of it, putting it down to Carol's shyness.

Carol decided that a change of subject was called for. Turning to Helen and the rest of the group she said, 'That was a good match last week!'

The Hopman Cup tennis tournament had just finished in Perth. Helen and Carol had followed their tennis favourites celebrating Federer's win once more.

'Ah, yes!' Helen broke in. 'Carol and I are away next week. We're off to Melbourne to watch the Australian Open finals.'

'Shall we still meet for cards?' Sharon asked, looking at Maggie and Camille.

'Well, I was meant to fly across to Melbourne next week, for a meeting. They want me to cover the launch of a new artist at one of the art galleries next month,' Camille explained.

'So you will be in Melbourne as well?' Helen asked, a coy look on her face.

'Actually ...probably not. I'm interviewing a

Perth philanthropist for next week, so I will try to move the Melbourne trip to two weeks later.

'Ok,' Sharon, the card game unofficial organiser said. 'Then how about we go ahead, just the three of us?'

'Yes. Definitely!' Camille replied.

'Good morning Sharon,' Camille started out, a few days later.

'Morning, Camille,' she answered. 'What's up?'

'The Perth assignment has been rescheduled, as the person I was to interview will be away. So I will be going to Melbourne after all. Leaving tomorrow. Sorry, but I won't be able to make it for cards this Thursday.'

'Oh, bad luck for us! Never mind. Maggie and I will just get together for a coffee then. Ah, and you may catch up with Helen and Carol.'

'Oh, I don't think so. Steve and I are both flying over for two days, as he also has some business to attend to. We have a busy schedule.' Steve was Camille's husband.

Camille and Steve flew out early the following morning. After a hectic afternoon with rounds of meetings, they looked forward to an early quiet meal at one of Melbourne's excellent fusion restaurants downtown. They had washed down a tasty meal of lobster rolls and chicken and prawn dumplings with some great Victorian Chardonnay: just right to lull them to sleep after a long day.

Camille and Steve strolled out of the restaurant into the busy street. Out of the corner of her eye, Camille saw another couple scrutinizing the menu outside the door of a restaurant, further down the street. She recognised Carol immediately. Carol and her husband looked like they were having fun, laughing and cuddling each other.

'Look, Steve. There's Carol and Patrick... Hang on. Something's not right.'

Camille looked more closely. 'Oh my goodness, that's not Patrick! That's Michael, Helen's husband,' she explained.

Carol and Michael had not seen them, and Camille quickly pulled Steve into the entrance of a nearby bistro.

'There they are, unmistakably smooching like a pair of teenagers! Oh goodness!' Camille muttered again, in shock. 'What on earth is going on? ...who would have thought! Quiet, careful Carol? ...and what do I do? I can't tell Helen!'

Thinking furiously, Camille and Steve turned back to take a different route to their hotel. They rounded the corner.

Camille was still shaking her head trying to take in what she had witnessed when she suddenly looked up - and almost bumped into – yes, really - Helen and Patrick, swaying cosily arm-in-arm!

Camille was not sure who was more stunned. Her eyes met Helen, and then she saw Helen's startled face start to relax as she gave Camille a sly cheeky wink!

'Hello Camille,' Helen said, undaunted. 'Fancy meeting you here!'

Camille had almost frozen in place, dazed and totally lost for words.

Steve took over.

'Hi guys!' he said as he pulled Camille along. 'Enjoy your meal. See you back in Perth!' he continued, as he walked away briskly, dragging his wife with him.

'Talk about mixed-doubles!' Steve whispered to Camille, as soon as they were out of earshot. Shaking his head, he continued. 'Darling, this is one secret you will have to take to your grave!'

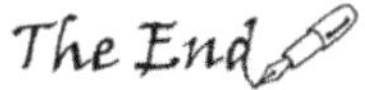

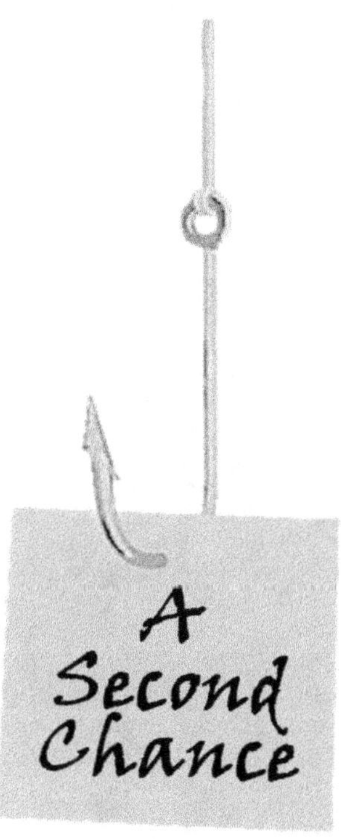
A
Second
Chance

William Robert Westlake - 'Bill' to his mates - migrated to Sydney in 2010, after the global financial crisis had plunged most of Europe into recession. An Information Technology (IT) professional in his early twenties, he secured a good position with one of the major Australian banks.

His career flourished and he soon found himself leading the IT division within the bank. The downside to this was the long hours and stress of the job, especially with the responsibility of ensuring the integrity of the bank's online services. Fatigue and muscular tension had become the order of the day, and lately he had started having sleeping difficulties.

'I feel I'm ageing prematurely,' he told his colleague and best mate Hamid, another IT professional who specialised in combating computer hacking. They were down at the local wine bar, enjoying a glass of Shiraz. 'There's got to be more to life than this.'

'Your problem is that your job has taken over your life. Most of the time, when we meet, we end up talking shop.'

'Yes. ...Sadly, true,' Bill reflected.

'Bill, you need to broaden your horizon. I think you should take time out to reassess your priorities.' Hamid smiled. 'I know you are on call 24/7 but that shouldn't stop you from taking up a hobby. You love the theatre – that's a good start. Perhaps take up a sport, go walking or join me in our cycling club. Get more active. Meet more people. Use the internet dating sites if necessary and go on dates. Your love life looks pretty dismal, you know.'

Bill gave his friend a long look. Hamid was earnest. More importantly, Bill could see that his friend was right. 'Ever since I arrived in Sydney, eight years ago, it has been all go' he replied. 'I was so happy to find a job I actually enjoyed – especially after our London IT firm closed down just six months after I had joined them. That had truly shaken me.'

Bill sat in thought, gently swirling the wine glass to draw oxygen from the air into the wine. He watched the so-called curtains form on the glass.

'I've been thinking of going on a return visit to the UK. A trip down memory lane to Oxford, where I grew up. Catch up with family. I haven't seen them since I got here. Perhaps catch up with some old friends too.'

With the amount of accumulated leave that he had, Bill had no problem arranging for a two-month holiday.

'It'll do you good Bill,' his superior had told him. 'Go and re-charge your batteries. You don't take enough time out and that's not good for you – or the company. As a director you should be leading by example, ensuring an appropriate work/life balance.'

The plane journey to London was long and tedious, but Bill managed some good stretches of sleep and arrived reasonably refreshed. He smartened himself up before the short train ride to Oxford. Then it was another taxi ride to his parents' home, where he was staying – at least to begin with.

As he stepped out onto the road to hail an approaching taxi, he was distracted and did not heed the traffic signals. He failed to spot the car that came speeding round the corner on a green turning light - until it was too late.

Bill was thrown back onto the pavement, hitting his head in the process. The next thing he knew he was waking up in the local hospital.

'Welcome back to the world,' someone greeted him.

'Where am I exactly? ...and what happened? Oooh ...my head throbs!' He looked up, confused, to see the gentle, concerned face of a nurse.

'You're in the John Radcliffe Hospital in Oxford. You're a lucky man. You were hit by a car and suffered concussion – but no major damage, apparently. The doctor will be along shortly to talk to you.'

Bill was mesmerised by the angel hovering over him. He read her nametag: Nurse Wilson. The first thing he noticed were the steely blue eyes that seemed to be drilling into him. The raven coloured hair tied back in a bob gave her a look of efficiency. This was somewhat softened by the slight roundedness of her face. He found her captivating.

'Oxford? Ah ...yes. Emm...I just got off a plane from Australia. I don't remember much else.'

'Australia? Just returned from a holiday?' she asked.

'No ...em.. I moved out there about eight years ago. I've come back to catch up with family...'

The doctor walked in at that very moment, interrupting the exchange. After greeting his patient, he told him, 'Glad to see you have come out of your concussion.'

The doctor examined Bill and asked several questions which Bill answered satisfactorily. 'You have been out for the best part of the day. All tests and the CT scan came out clear. You have multiple injuries, including a nasty bump on your head and a broken leg, but nothing that a good rest won't heal. Of course, we'll keep you under observation for a few days. The orthopaedic surgeon will be in later. He'll advise you on your leg injury. You're in good hands here.' He paused, checked his notes, and then added, 'Em... we have been trying to work out your next-of-kin. Luckily, your parents made contact with us via the police. They should be here soon.'

As the doctor took his leave, Bill turned his attention once again to the nurse. He was about to state that it seemed he would be lingering in the hospital for a few days. Yet strangely enough, she abruptly left the room.

Clare Wilson walked back to the nurse's desk, deep in thought.

'What's up?' asked Mandy, noticing the frown on Clare's face. Mandy was more than a colleague; she was Clare's close friend. They also shared an apartment.

'It's nothing,' Clare replied, rather tersely.

Something in Clare's look told Mandy that it

was no use pushing for information at this stage. However, she decided that she would keep a close lookout for her friend.

The days passed slowly for Bill. He was aware of Nurse Wilson, glasses permanently perched on the edge of her nose, checking on him day and night whenever she was on duty. He found himself greatly drawn to her, yet he was puzzled by her behaviour. He could sense that she seemed to care more than was usual. 'Perhaps she shares my feelings,' he mused. Then he dismissed the thought as she became even more cool and distant in his presence.

As he recovered and his leg healed, he noticed that Clare Wilson – he had asked another nurse for her name – was more and more withdrawn with him. At the same time, he was sure she was keeping a close eye on his progress, and more than the call of duty required.

Mandy noticed Clare's behaviour whenever she left Bill's ward.

'What's up Clare? Every time you've been in to check on Westlake, you walk out with ... I don't know what to call it ...a troubled look?

...Anger? Something is bothering you or getting to you. You know you can trust me. What's going on?'

Clare looked at her friend, and held her breath. 'Ah, Mandy,' she started out, lifting her hand as though to brush her hair - and her cares away. 'Where do I start? I'm due for my lunch break so let's go get a coffee.'

Clare collected her thoughts carefully.

'About nine years ago,' she started out, 'I was at the Turf – you know the tavern next to the University – and I finally got to meet this handsome guy I had been admiring from a distance. I was with a group of friends and he caught my eye. He finally plucked up enough courage to prise me from my friends. We chatting away happily, and then he asked me out. We spent a wonderful evening really hitting it off! I even went to bed with him – something I never do on a first date! He was vivacious, suitably flirty, and had a good sense of humour - and I guess I really fell for him.' Clare paused to catch her breath. She shook her head as though trying to shrug off her misgivings.

'In the morning, he was really charming and engaging. He got up early and rushed out to get some fresh croissants for breakfast. He seemed so keen. He took my contact details, entering them on his cell phone and then promised to call me back later in the day.'

Mandy listened without interrupting, a concerned look on her face.

'Well, he never called back. I returned to the same pub a number of times, but I never saw him again. ...Until now, that is. There he is lying in my ward, under my care and he doesn't seem to remember me!' Clare paused. 'I'm baffled. It's as if we've never met before. I feel as though I was invisible. ...I feel so used. Used and abused. To make matters worse, I swear he's trying to chat me up.'

'Ouch!' Mandy started out. 'And you're sure it's the same guy.'

'I wasn't sure when he said he had just flown in from Australia. But then he told me that he left the UK about eight years ago. ...And his family live around here. He looks the same – perhaps slightly older. ...And a bit more serious – not as carefree. Age does that sometimes. I'm sure it's him. I remember he introduced himself very formally. And let's face it; there are not many Westlakes around Oxford.'

'What a pig!'

'That's not the worst part,' Clare continued. 'I can't help but feel drawn to him.' Clare rubbed her brow and then swept her fingers through her hair. 'And I feel that I'm falling for him all over again! I'm so disgusted with myself.'

'Oh my! I don't know what to say. Why don't you check again with Laki about the possibility of memory loss?'

Clare decided to take Mandy's advice. She approached her colleague, Dr Laki Pradesh.

'Is it possible that Westlake has suffered some sort of amnesia?' Clare asked the doctor. 'We met about eight years ago – well ...we had a great time together, but he seems to have no recollection of our having met. I don't think I've changed that much that I would be unrecognisable. In fact, I think I've hardly changed at all.'

'I've given him the all clear, Clare. And no, there seems to be no sign of memory loss.'

Bill could not understand why it was so difficult to engage in any conversation with Clare. He wondered if she was married and if that was the reason for her reticence. He tried to raise the subject of families with her, but Clare was having none of it.

When he was about to be discharged, he decided to take the bull by the horns and ask her out.

'Nurse Wilson – Clare,' He started out hesitantly. 'I would really like to get to know you. Look, if you're married or have a partner, I understand and I'll keep away. But I can't fathom why you are so distant with me.'

Clare looked him in the eye. She was taken aback. Bill had spoken with such earnestness. What she saw was honesty. This man clearly did not know – or could not remember - who she was.

An emotional tug of war was going on inside her as to whether to accept going on a date. On the one hand, there was the hurt that a wonderful and memorable evening that had left such a mark on her life could have been so insignificant to the other party. On the other, she was attracted to him and curious to find out why he had never called her back.

'Let me think about it,' she replied, and

walked out.

<><><>

Clare approached the ward where Bill lay in bed. She hesitated for a minute, and then resolutely walked in.

'Ok,' she told him. 'I'll go on a date with you. How about the Turf Tavern? I'm off work in the next two days. Would lunch on Friday suit?' She hoped that perhaps the venue would prod his memory.

Bill was surprised and a bit shocked by her abrupt behaviour. Yet his pleasure at her acceptance won over. For a fleeting minute, he considered his crutches and hoped the pub in question was accessible.

'Great!' he said. 'See you Friday. I'll be there!'

<><><>

Clare arrived at the appointed time at the pub to find that Bill had arrived early and found a table outdoors. It was a balmy and sunny June day. To start with, they fell into pleasant conversation. He told her about migrating to Australia and his life – and work - in Sydney.

'I'm afraid I let my work dominate my life.

The one pleasurable break was going to the theatre. And Sydney offers a varied repertoire.' He paused, then continued, 'In fact, this trip was about rethinking my life: there has to be more to it than just work.' And he gave her a smile, hopeful that Clare would be as responsive.

'I've never been to Australia.' Clare replied. 'It must be wonderful to walk into the iconic Sydney Opera House. I find nursing rewarding, but the theatre is my greatest love. I do enjoy a good ballet or opera.'

Clare was disappointed that even their shared love of the theatre had not survived his recollections. Bill was considerate and pleasant: not as bubbly or as carefree as she remembered – in fact he seemed more serious and perhaps a bit nerdy. Somehow, she found him even more appealing.

'By the way, why do you call yourself by your second name?' she asked, unexpectedly.

'My second name?' he replied, confused.

'Yes. - Ah well...' Clare paused to pull her hair back, and then took the plunge. 'I have a confession to make. We have met before. About eight, maybe nine, years ago. And it was here, at this pub, that we met.'

Bill looked at her, clearly bewildered.

'I'm sure I would remember if I had met you before.' He stopped to reflect on what she had said. Then he added, 'And what's this about my name?'

'It was so odd that I remember it clearly. You introduced yourself as Robert William Westlake. Not many people use their full name when introducing themselves.'

Bill took his time to digest this. 'Hang on... I don't remember ever meeting you before... would never have let you go... did you say Robert? ...Oh no!'

Unexpectedly, the penny dropped! It was as if a bolt of lightning – or rather, enlightenment – had struck. He suddenly understood her behaviour and the confusing conversation they were having.

'Clare,' he started out, reaching over to hold her hand. 'I'm a twin. An identical twin. I'm William Robert ...and my brother is Robert William.' He reached into his wallet, rummaged around a bit, and then brought out a worn photo of the two brothers. You could not tell them apart – not at first glance, anyway.

'It used to happen a lot when I was younger and still lived here in Oxford. In the end, I carried this photo because some people were sceptical – thought I was pulling their leg. It has become a part of my wallet.

'Eight years in Sydney and I forgot all about being mistaken for my brother.' Then he continued. 'Now I think of it, just before I left I remember Bob complaining about losing his cell phone under the wheel of a bus – he went on endlessly about losing someone's telephone number. ...By the way, Bob is now married with two young boys I'm hoping to meet soon.'

Clare was left speechless. It took more than a minute or two before she could reply. What an idiot she had been! The first clear thought that entered her mind was that she'd been given a second chance – with Bill.

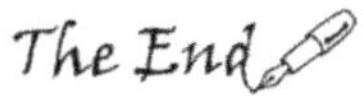

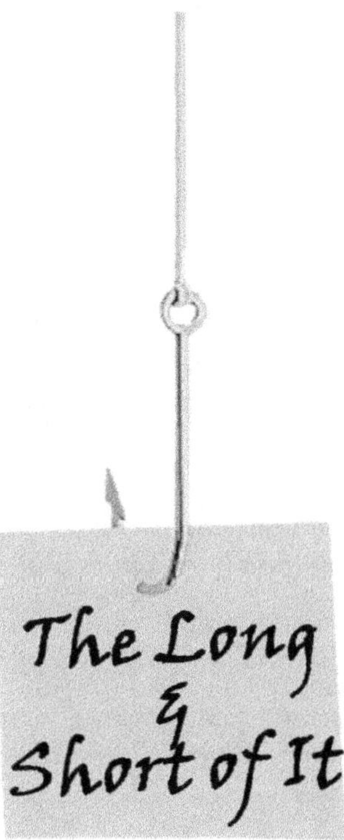
The Long
&
Short of It

She was sitting on her soft couch, knitting away, and watching the evening news. Kirsten was in her mid-sixties, a mop of cropped blond, curly hair atop an attractive and innocent-looking face with gentle green eyes. To the casual observer, here was your favourite gran, a homebody knitting away peacefully, whiling away the evening.

Kirsten had enjoyed a delicious dinner with her daughter Clara. They had a close relationship. Clara visited on a regular basis, often coming over to her mother on her scooter with her life partner Agnete. Thus time, however, Clara had come alone.

'Agnete has to study for her nursing exams next week,' Clara had explained to her mum. 'I'm sure she will do well, but you know how she is. She gets so anxious.'

'To be honest I never liked exams,' Kirsten said. 'So I can well understand. But she has missed out on the meatballs tonight.'

'When she knew what you were cooking she almost changed her mind. But she sends her love.'

'And I'll put some aside for you to take home,' laughed Kirsten.

It was now nearing 9.00pm.

'Time for a cup of tea - and perhaps a little tot of brandy?' Kirsten asked Clara.

'No brandy for me. I'm on my scooter.'

Just then, Clara's phone rang. 'It's Agnete,' she said to her mother as she walked out to the living room to take the call.

Kirsten headed into the kitchen. With summer approaching, it was still twilight in Copenhagen, Denmark at that hour. Kirsten casually looked out of the large bay windows that overlooked the laneway to their house as she carefully poured hot water into the teapot.

Then she looked again!

'Hey YOU!' she screamed, as loudly as she could, whilst knocking on the double-glazed glass pane. 'Clara! Come! Quick!'

Clara threw down the phone, leaving Agnete hanging on the other side of the line.

'What's wrong, mum?' she said as she scurried into the kitchen.

'Someone just stole your scooter. From right under my nose... right outside the kitchen window!' she said, full of indignation. 'He had an accomplice, another tall guy. I saw them arrive, and then one of them got off and went over to your scooter. It took him no time at all to get it started.'

'Oh no!'

'Quick! Get your shoes on! Come on!'

Clara knew better than to question her mum when she was on a mission – as she so obviously was. She followed her mother out of the house and jumped into Kirsten's little car. She had hardly had time to put her belt on before Kirsten took off, wheels almost spinning.

Kirsten turned into the main road. 'See if you can spot them. They can't be far ahead of us.'

They came to a T-junction. 'There's no way they would go on to a highway,' Kirsten mumbled, steam practically rising out of her ears. She took a right hand turn instead and hooned down the road, struggling to stick to the speed limit. As she approached the red light ahead, she slammed on the brakes.

'Look mum,' shouted an excited Clara. 'Good call! There they are – about to turn left, down there.' Clara pointed to the road to their left. She sneaked a look at her usually quiet, gentle mama, now transformed into a determined avenger, muttering in disgust, furious at the brazen theft.

A green light saw wheels spinning and burning tyres as Kirsten took off. Clara watched transfixed. She had never seen her mother so thoroughly pissed off!

Kirsten drove towards the stolen scooter, and caught sight of his accomplice just further ahead. When she almost caught up with the thief, she put her hand on the car horn, blaring away and waking up the silent neighbourhood.

Lights came on along the street, deserted except for the incredible car-scooter chase that was taking place.

What happened next was a remarkable sight. Careful not to endanger the thieves, Kirsten drove ahead of them and then cut them off. She flung the car door open, jumped out and gave chase, followed by an equally wound up and angry Clara.

'You thieves! You cheeky people! How dare you!' Kirsten shouted in outrage, shaking her fist in the air.

'Give me back my scooter!' Clara hollered in accompaniment, adding to the din as more lights came on behind curtained windows.

The accomplice managed to swerve his scooter around the car and escape. The thief, on Clara's scooter, hesitated. Being further back, his only choice was to turn around, as two determined women blocked his way forward.

Little gran was no more! This ball of energy came whooshing towards him. Little did he know that he had thrown down the gauntlet to a marathon runner. Despite the fact that he was still in his teens, young and healthy, he quickly realised that her deceptive appearance disguised her agility.

<><><>

'What's going on here?' The resident of the house stepped out to investigate. In his front yard stood the stolen scooter and an unfolding confrontation.

He could not believe his eyes. What he saw was an elderly woman, barely nudging 5 feet chasing a man almost twice her size - and catching up!. The thief took off down the garden to escape via the back yards in the neighbourhood.

Kirsten stopped dead in her tracks. The would-be thief was on private property and, although she had been catching up on him, he was now on private property with the owner challenging them.

Clara meanwhile ran over to claim her abandoned scooter. 'He stole my scooter! Mum saw him out of the kitchen window, called out to me and we gave chase,' she gasped breathlessly.

'Okay, take a deep breath and calm down. I'm a police officer. Now tell me what happened.'

'You tell him what happened while I go home and retrieve the scooter keys,' Kirsten said, leaving Clara and the scooter in the capable care of the officer.

Kirsten returned with the keys, so her daughter could drive the scooter home.

'Do you want to put in a report?' the officer asked.

'Not much point,' answered Kirsten. 'We got the scooter back.'

Kirsten and Clara returned home. Clara took her scooter to the shed in the back yard rather than leaving it on the street.

'I definitely need a drink after that.' Kirsten said. She headed into the kitchen to resume where she had left off before her routine had been so rudely interrupted. She put the kettle on, and poured herself a little tot of brandy. Then she made her way to the comfortable couch and took up her knitting once more.

Kirsten suddenly caught a movement out of the corner of her eyes and spotted a dark shape on her back veranda, which was followed by a face looking in.

'What now!' she thought aloud. She got up and looked more closely. A woman was signalling to her to open the door and let her in. A closer look showed that this woman was a police officer.

Kirsten opened the door, a puzzled look on her face. She invited the female police officer and her male partner in.

'Hello! What's happening? Why are you at my back door?' Kirsten asked, puzzled.

'Are you Clara?'

'No, I'm Kirsten, her mum.' Kirsten called out to her daughter to join her. 'This is my daughter, Clara,' she said by way of introduction.

The police woman turned to Clara 'Are you all right?'

'Yes, I am. I don't understand? Why are you here?'

'We got a call from a very distressed young woman claiming that her friend Clara – and probably her mother - was being attacked, and that your lives could be in danger.'

Clara paused for a second. 'Ah ...my partner, Agnete. I was on the phone with her when you called out, mum. It was all panic. And I forgot to hang up.'

'Well, you had better tell us what happened,' the police officer said.

Kirsten took over. She was still mad at the

audacity of the theft, and related the whole episode with gusto. As she recounted the chain of events, she noticed the police woman's' eyes widen in disbelief.

...And who could blame her? The police woman was trying to reconcile the image of the vertically challenged, seemingly harmless dear old lady knitting away whom she had seen through the veranda window, with the speed chase, screeching tyres and hooting, and finally the confrontation with two young, tall thieves.

After hearing the full story, she was sure that out there that night were two traumatised would-be robbers trying to dismiss the image of an outraged, diminutive gran, steam coming out of her ears, giving chase in a car and on foot, and raising her fist at them.

...And that was the Long and the Short of it!

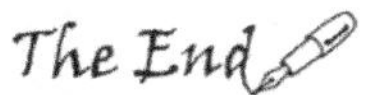

Dressing
Gowns &
Diversions

She nervously knocked on the door.

'Nicole. ...Come in!'

Nicole looked at Jessica in amusement. It was almost midday and she was still wearing her bathrobe. Or should it be called a dressing gown, since Jessica seemed to don this for lounging around the house at all times of the day.

'I've just come out of the shower. I've been to the gym for my pump class this morning.'

Nicole smiled. Dear Jessica. Nicole knew that her friend was marking time in Bunbury, a small city some 200 kilometres south of Perth. Jessica hailed from London, but had been living in Texas where she had attended university, graduating in clinical sexology - a profession she was loathe to broadcast in social gatherings. It usually meant that women buzzed around her like a honeypot, seeking to elicit some juicy sexual tips. The men were more discreet, but no less interested. And of course, there was always the idiot who offered their 'services' for - shall we say - research purposes, given her professional interest.

Jessica had met her husband Dave at university. Dave was a chemical engineer and worked for a multinational petro-chemical company. He had been posted to one of the company's alumina refineries in Western Australia's south-west for two years. Three years down the track, Jessica and David were still living in Bunbury. Much as Jessica loved to explore the vast continent, and the occasional forays into the wild and exciting northwest of the State, the adventure of living in a small, regional city had fizzled out. She missed the buzz and exhilaration of city life bustling with activity, especially when it came to nightlife and the arts.

'Put the kettle on while I finish drying my hair.' Jessica's reddish brown hair complemented her very English complexion to the extent that even her freckles added to the vitality in her face. There was always a twinkle lurking there, especially when she smiled.

'Where do you keep the decaf tea nowadays? I presume that you still indulge in that insipid brew,' Nicole called out.

Nicole fumbled around in the kitchen. Her mind drifted because this was no pure, social visit. If anything, she had come on a fact-finding mission.

Her bubbly friend had been showing signs of restlessness lately. Every week she begged Nicole to accompany her to Perth, sometimes forgetting that Nicole's two boys, aged five and three respectively, had a routine that was often difficult to plan around.

It would have helped if Jessica had been able to resume to her career. However, as an expatriate - and given the nature of her profession - it had proved to be an impossible situation in conservative Bunbury.

Then a week ago, Nicole's raffish jet setting cousin, Peter, turned up unexpectedly. Without a second thought, Nicole introduced her favourite cousin to her best friend, hoping that Peter would help cheer Jessica up.

Jessica's reaction had been more than a murmur of approval. 'I've heard so much about you,' she playfully told Peter.

'Hmm... but the question is, why has Nicole kept you hidden away?' Peter inquired, a broad, wicked grin on his face.

Jessica and Peter warmed to each other immediately. They seemed to be in accord, and Nicole was delighted that they got on so well. Yet Nicole was surprised when Jessica revealed her profession to him.

'A sexologist?' Peter had remarked. To Nicole's amazement, Peter did not make the usual jokes, or pull Jessica's leg. He seemed genuinely fascinated. 'Tell me about it.'

Nicole floundered. Both Jessica and Peter were behaving out of character. Jessica usual reluctance to discuss her profession was gone, and her friend chatted away merrily on some of the more humorous aspects of her work. This was unheard of, as Jessica took her profession seriously. The normally flippant Peter, on the other hand, had been respectful, listening to

Jessica with interest.

Peter was in Bunbury for a week or two. Given the success of their first encounter, the three of them met on an almost daily basis. Whenever Nicole had to attend to her family, Jessica offered to take Peter around.

At first, Nicole was delighted. She had watched the harmless flirtation with amusement. Now she was not sure. There was no doubt that Peter's company had helped bring about Jessica's upbeat mood. However, as the days flew by, she sensed that something else was going on. Then Peter suddenly went up to Perth.

'Here you are: decaf tea! If you are into health drinks, why don't you try herbal infusions instead? How can you even drink this?' Nicole said.

Nicole was addicted to coffee, the stronger the better. Clutching her steaming mug, she looked up at her friend and continued. 'I've decided to go up to Perth tomorrow and help Peter out. I've rearranged my schedule and a friend is looking after the children.' Nicole sipped at her coffee, and then added, 'He has this crazy idea of buying an apartment before returning to Europe at the end of next week. It will be fun to have a *pied-a-terre* that I can borrow in Perth - not that I can see when he will get to use it. Why don't you come along too? I'm sure that he will not mind.'

Jessica looked up, fleetingly, almost guiltily.

'Actually I had already planned to go up to Perth. Peter phoned and said that you had abandoned him. He asked me to help him out.'

On the face of it, it looked innocent enough - except for the fact that Peter knew Nicole's schedule, and that she was usually unavailable on Wednesdays.

Nicole's heart sank. 'Perhaps I should never have brought them together,' she chided herself. To add to the intrigue, since meeting Jessica, Peter had asked some seemingly casual but probing questions about her friend.

Nicole tried to tell herself that it was none of her business. Peter was thirty-three, handsome and too well off for his own good. He was a bit of a rake and led an unpredictable lifestyle, gallivanting around the world. Then he would grow bored and restless. That was usually when he came to visit Nicole and her family. Different though they were, there was a strong bond between them.

Nicole knew Peter was incorrigible when it came to women - and Jessica being her friend made her even more enticing. She worried that Jessica should be off limits and her present state of boredom could easily lead her to mischief.

'Great!' Nicole lied, coming back into the present. 'Let's go up together. I'll pick you up at eight. I also have some shopping to do in the afternoon.'

Jessica's smile was as enigmatic as that of the Sphinx!

<><><>

The next morning went as planned. It was a lovely, sunny, but cool day, beautiful weather for the two-hour drive to Perth. The girls chatted away aimlessly most of the way, except for when the conversation drifted to Peter's errant life.

'He says he wants to settle down, but I doubt he knows how to.'

'Maybe he hasn't met the right person so far.'

'The right person doesn't just step into your life. If you are always on the move, it is very difficult to have a stable relationship. You also have to accept the give-and-take that goes with it - something that I am not too sure Peter knows the meaning of.'

'You may be reading more into it than is necessary. Some people take their time to find the right partner – if that's what he's after,' Jessica offered.

'Well, there's his family background: a bully for a dad, and a meek mum that was intimidated until she was only a shadow of her former self. Her death when he was at the tender age of twelve removed the only affection he has known from his immediate family. I know how badly it affected him.'

Nicole broke off to negotiate overtaking a campervan on the narrow road. Then she resumed her commentary.

'Leaving his father's business empire and branching out on his own was a step in the right direction. He's done well for himself, but a flippant approach to life also means that he can sometimes be a little bit selfish and reckless.'

'He certainly seems sure of himself. I just love his cheeky sense of humour.'

'True. We've had some great times together over the years. He's such fun to have around, and the kids adore him.' Nicole paused, before adding thoughtfully, 'Sometimes, though, I feel that it has become one huge act - this endless partying all over the globe.'

'I know you are fond of him but I think you are being over-protective. He is genuinely good company and seems quite sensible and grounded.'

The trio met up and had an early lunch at one of Fremantle's outdoor cafes, overlooking the harbour. Peter was his usual amiable self, amusing them with his latest exploits.

'Well. I'm off. I have a long list of shopping to go through.' Turning to Peter, Nicole continued, 'you won't need me with Jessica along. She knows her way around Perth better than I do. What time shall we meet, and where?'

'The estate agent is meeting us here, in Fremantle. He recommended about three hours. Ample time eh, Nicole?' Peter grinned wickedly, winking at his cousin. He knew Nicole well enough to realise she was concerned about his behaviour. 'How about four o'clock? We can come into town and meet you if that is where you will end up.'

'Fine. Corner Hay and William at 4pm. See you later ...and don't get lost in the bedrooms!' Nicole was not going to let Peter get away with his teasing.

Nicole left them sipping their cappuccinos. 'What a gorgeous day!' she thought to herself. Lunch had been fun and lively. She had enjoyed the light-hearted banter and Peter had been his usual self: charming, impeccable manners, and full of humour. He was excited at the prospect of owning property in Perth. Anyway, she reasoned, Jessica was a grown-up woman, in her early thirties, and sensible. Accompanying Peter around gave her something to do, especially as she enjoyed looking around at property - a task Nicole had not relished.

Nicole turned her attention to her husband's list: electronic bits and bobs, a book or two on the classics, and short-sleeved shirts. 'Men!' she said to herself. As usual, it was going to be an endless rush from store to store until she found what she presumed he was after - especially the books. As she only worked part-time, teaching

English mostly to new arrivals in Australia, her husband believed that she had nothing better to do in her spare time other than run around chasing after his errands. He seemed to forget their two high-energy sons and the endless demands on her time.

'Goodness, it's past four!' Nicole exclaimed as she rushed to keep her rendezvous.

'Sorry I'm late!' She puffed, armed with a number of parcels that swung against her legs and threatened to trip her.

'Bought out the entire city, have you?' joked Peter. 'Here, let me take those,' he continued, as he reached out for her bags.

'Definitely coffee time. I'm exhausted. How was your afternoon?'

'There are some lovely, picturesque spots along the river,' Peter started out. 'Quite a few places for sale to choose from.'

'Then we saw a lovely apartment in Mosman Park. It had fantastic views – you can see both the river and the beach. It was a bit pricy, but not exorbitant...' Jessica hesitated, and then she looked coyly at Nicole and continued: 'I'm staying in Perth tonight. I'll come down tomorrow with Peter.'

'What! ..eh..yes...of course.' Nicole stuttered, unable to hide her astonishment. She could not resist asking, 'what is going on?'

'I asked her to,' Peter broke in. 'I was thinking of coming back down to Bunbury tonight, but the estate agent wants to show us one more apartment. Jessica has been invaluable company - very patient and observant. So I suggested one more viewing followed by dinner.'

'Dave doesn't mind?'

'Oh no. I'll probably stay with Jan overnight.' Jan was a girlfriend of theirs.

'Fine. Well then, have a good time and see you tomorrow.'

With a hug for Jessica and a peck on Peter's cheek, Nicole left.

The drive back to Bunbury was monotonous, to say the least. Nicole had to stop herself from speeding - both mentally, as her thoughts raced in all sorts of directions with negative implications, and physically, as she noticed the speedometer registering over 120 miles per hour. She knew it was ridiculous to feel responsible for two adults. She cared about Peter and Jessica deeply, and felt angry with them both. Beyond all the joking, Nicole sensed that they were playing with fire, especially as she knew that Jessica was happily married to Dave. She could not see a positive conclusion to this episode.

Nicole was irritable all evening and she slept badly that night, tossing and turning until eventually, she woke up in a cold sweat. 'Where's my wife?' Dave was asking insistently in her dreams.

The phone rang.

'Hello!'

'Morning,' said a rather cheerful Peter. 'Sorry cus! I have to leave for Hong Kong immediately.'

'We won't be seeing you then?' Nicole asked. She was disappointed. Peter was such good company and Jake, her five year old, had been looking forward to spending time with him.

'Not for a few weeks anyway. I have to go to Europe afterwards, but I will be back as soon as possible. The last apartment Jessica and I saw was a bit of a disappointment. I am determined to purchase a property in Perth, but it will have to wait.'

'Peter…' Nicole hesitated.

Nicole could almost hear his soft laughter as, instead of explanations or elaboration, Peter continued casually. 'Jessica is taking the train down tonight. I sent some gifts for Jake and Matt. Take care!'

'Oh thanks. The boys will like that. Do call, and let us know what's going on, Have a good trip you so-and-so!'

It was Saturday afternoon and Nicole had not heard from Jessica in two days. The boys were off fishing with their dad and so Nicole decided to drive round to Jessica's house. She was apprehensive as she knocked on the front door.

It took a minute or two to elicit a response.

'Nicole! Hello …er…come in. I was coming over later this afternoon. Peter sent some gifts for the boys, and for you and Mike too.'

Nicole had to hide the smile that threatened. 'This woman was unbelievable,' she thought. 'Not in her dressing gown again! It was 3.30pm for goodness sake!'

Nicole was suddenly aware of Dave in the background, hairy legs sticking out of his dressing gown, and with ruffled hair and an unmistakable twinkle in his eyes. Jessica's flushed face suddenly had new meaning. Whatever had happened in Perth had not affected her home love life – not negatively at least! Nicole could not miss the amusement in Jessica's eyes, and felt sure there was a connection somewhere.

'No thanks,' Nicole responded, half-laughing, half-sighing with relief. 'It seems the two of you are kind of busy...'

With that, she waltzed off into the afternoon sun, a huge smile on her face.

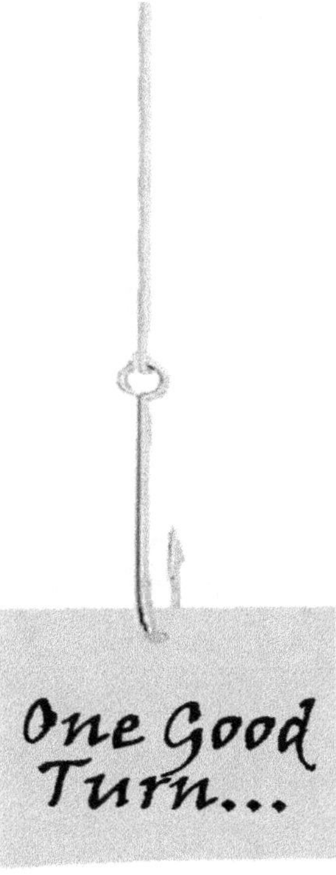
One Good
Turn...

Most people dream of living and working in Paris but for Marie, a Parisienne by birth, it was a different story.

She was just fourteen years of age when her *Grand'Mere* died. *Grand'Mere* had lived with her family for as long as she could remember. Marie remembered her fondly, her rosy cheeks crowned with an unruly mob of white hair that *Grand'Mere* always tried to tame with hairpins and tortoiseshell combs. *Grand'Mere* was plump and wore no colour but black. Despite this, she came across as a gentle angel, always ready with a smile and a hug. Marie's first memory of her childhood was of *Grand'Mere*'s morning routine when she would gently comb out Marie's long hair and plait it in readiness for another day at school.

'Ma chouchoute,' Grand'Mere would tell Marie. 'When you grow up you must visit Guadeloupe, where I was born, and where your mother grew up. It is a beautiful island where the birds sing to you every morning, and the turquoise sea calls to you to play in it. I have a house there, and this is for you when you grow up.'

Saddened as she was when her *Grand'Mere* passed away, Marie soon forgot about her promise of the house in the Caribbean island of Guadeloupe. She finished high school, and went on to a training institute to take up hairdressing. In order to fund her way, Marie took a job with her *Tante* Juliette who ran a store that specialised in an eclectic array of gifts and goods. Her store rang with a continuous flow of advice about which herbs, tinctures, and oils from her well-stocked shop to apply in various situations. *Tante* Juliette was the local herbalist in the quarter where Marie's family lived.

Marie loved hairdressing. She had found a job at one of the local salons. Handling other people's hair always brought back fond memories of her *Grand'Mere*. 'Tonight I must ask *Maman* about the house that *Grand'Mere* always spoke to me about,' she would say to herself. Yet after a long day on her feet, often followed by a few hours helping her *Tante* Juliette at the herb shop, she was so exhausted that she would plain forget to mention anything to her mother.

Until her mother brought up the subject herself, that is.

'Marie, I have received a letter from my brother, your *Oncle* Henri in Guadeloupe,' Amélie began, over dinner one evening.

Marie looked up expectantly as her mother continued, '*Grand tante* Margarethe has died. It seems that the house she was living in belonged to *Grand'Mere*. But now that she is gone, it passes down to you.'

'The house that *Grand'Mere* used to tell me about?' Marie queried. 'I've been meaning to ask you about it, but I always forget by the time I get home.' Marie paused to let the news sink in. 'I wasn't sure if it was true. I thought it was just another story.'

<><><>

The house in Guadeloupe would not leave Marie's thoughts. During the day, at the salon, her clients would often notice that something else was on her mind, as she suddenly lost track of the conversation.

'*Coucou*, Marie? Where are you? What are you thinking about?' Most of Marie's clients were regulars who knew Marie and her family well.

'Ah *pardon*! *Grand'Mere* left me her house after she died. It's in Guadeloupe. *Grand'Mere* loved the island where she grew up, and I think she missed it terribly. I can't stop thinking about it. I feel drawn to it like a magnet.'

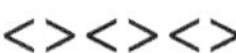

Marie was on a mission. She saved hard to be able to afford the trip to the Caribbean island. Within a year, she was within sight of her goal.

'I have booked a ticket to Guadeloupe,' Marie told her *Maman*. 'And I have arranged to have two months' holiday. I want to find out all about the island, and the places *Grand'Mere* used to talk to me about.'

'Where will you be staying? Did you write to

Oncle Henri?'

'Yes, I did. He said that I should stay with him. Then he can show me around, and tell me all about the island's history and especially the village where he and *Grand'Mere*'s remaining family still live.'

'Your *Oncle* Henri is a very kind man. You will like him.'

The trip to the Caribbean island of Guadeloupe changed her life. *Oncle* Henri was there to greet her at the airport, photo in hand to make sure he recognised his now grown-up niece. Her pink streaked hair threw him off to begin with, but there was no mistaking her smile, so like her mother's.

'*Bienvenue*!' he told her. Marie hugged the uncle she was meeting for the first time.

'*Maman* sends all her love. She told me I had to tell her all about you, the village, and the island. I know she also misses it. ...And I have to call her every day. Do you have internet, *Oncle*?'

'*Mais oui*,' Henri replied. He put Marie's suitcase in his ancient but reliable Citroën *deux-chevaux*. He then drove them to his home in a small town in the southern part of Grande-Terre. It was a few streets away from the charming bungalow Marie had inherited.

Marie did not waste time and the next day she walked over with her uncle to the bungalow.

'It's so charming!' she exclaimed. As she walked around, examining every room, she could see that it was well furnished and had that cosy lived-in feeling. It had that retro look about it that she loved. She could practically move in.

'It may need a few repairs,' Henri told her. 'But I can help. I have been looking after this place while Margarethe lived here. I know it well.'

'It's as if time has stood still,' Marie said. 'And there's everything I would need to live here.'

'*Mais non*, stay with me for now. Then once you have decided what you want to do with the property, we can talk about it.'

Over the course of the first week, Henri took Marie around to see the rest of the butterfly shaped island. Henri took her to meet other members of the extended family. He introduced her to many of the local people who made her feel welcome, often asking after her mother, aware that her dad had passed away a few years back.

Marie loved walking down the main road of the little village. Soon she could recognise many of the locals. She found herself falling in love with the island and its people. Her uncle was a goldmine of information, and always ready and willing to help. She visited her bungalow almost daily, spending several pleasant hours going through what was there. Then she would Skype her mother to relate every single detail of the day.

A month flew by, and Marie knew that she did not want to leave the island.

'I so love it here,' Marie told her mother, on one of her daily chats. '*Oncle* Henri and everyone have made me feel welcome. But I know I will miss you terribly.'

'*Chérie*, you have to make your own life.' Amélie said. Then she added, 'I will miss you too, but it would not be good if you returned and later regretted your decision. Don't go through life wondering "what if".'

A week later Marie finally made up her mind.

She approached her uncle. 'I have decided to stay – for now, at least. Give it a go. But first I must do something about work.'

'That's great news! What are you thinking of doing? How can I help?'

'Well I will try and get a job as a hairdresser in Sainte Anne.' Sainte Anne was a nearby city. 'But I would love to open my own place. There is no hairdressing salon in the village,' Marie continued, 'so perhaps I can convert the little garage or one of the rooms in the bungalow – at least to begin with.'

'Hmm, give me some time,' Henri continued. 'I think I have an idea.'

Two hectic days later, during which time Henri spoke to the mayor and a number of villagers, Henri got home to a lovely stew that Marie had cooked. 'I've been giving your idea a lot of thought,' he started out excitedly. 'I think I have a plan that may work.'

'I can't wait to hear all about it. I have hardly seen you the past two days. I knew you were up to something,' Marie smiled, excitedly.

'Well, I spoke to Bridgette, the *Maire*, about your plans - she's an old friend - and very helpful. She thought a salon in the village would be very welcome, but she warned that the bungalow was not the way to go. It is too out-of-the-way.'

'Oh really! Emm... I guess she's right. What did she suggest?' Marie felt deflated.

'Somewhere in the main street would be best. It would bring in the clients and help you get established more quickly.'

'I'm sure she's right. But I can't afford to rent such a place. And of course, we don't know if anything is available.'

'That's where my plan comes in,' Henri smiled conspiratorially. 'I love having you around and l enjoy being able to help. So why don't you stay on with me for now. One condition though: drop the '*Oncle*'. From now on it's 'Henri' please.' Henri pretended to look at Marie sternly. 'Then you can rent your bungalow. It's on the outskirts of the village, but also closer to the beach. You can get good rent – especially from visitors to the island. You can list it with the tourist bureau.'

'I can see where you are going,' Marie brightened up. 'With the rental income, I can afford to pay for a property in the main street. But is anywhere available?'

'Oh yes. Bridgette suggested I speak to Alphonse at the general store. I did. He has a warehouse further along the street that is empty, probably larger than you need, but we can always do something about that. When I explained your plans, he was enthusiastic. He thought that more facilities would increase the local business. And Bridgette is keen to encourage more enterprise in the village.' Henri paused for breath. 'The best is yet to come. The warehouse has been unused for some time and is empty, so Alphonse is happy for you to have it at a very low rent.'

'Oh, you have been busy! That's fantastic news!' Marie was almost in tears as she ran to give her uncle a big hug.

Marie could not wait to finish dinner to call her mother to tell her the terrific news. '*Maman*,' she started out. '*Oncle* Henri has been such a treasure.' When she finished recounting all that had happened, she continued. 'And Henri is also going to help me get the salon ready and act as a guarantor for the bank loan to do the place up!'

'*Chérie*, I am so happy for you,' Amélie said. 'I must write to Henri and thank him profusely. He's a good man and a kind soul. It's good to know he is looking after you.'

It took Marie about two months to get the salon ready. With Henri by her side, she located all the appropriate trades and cajoled them to finish the work as soon as possible. Bridgette was delighted to do the honours and open the first salon in the village. The clients began to call in, slowly at first, cautious of the bubbly newcomer with the pink hair. However, with the Mayor as one of Marie's first satisfied clients, word soon spread that the hairdresser at *Top Coiff* was not only very good, but also well priced.

Within a few months, Marie had a regular clientele. As her financial situation began to improve, she employed an assistant.

'How is it going?' Bridgette asked Marie on one of her weekly visits to the salon to get her hair done.

'It's perfect!' a delighted Marie answered. 'The salon is busy and the villagers are so supportive.'

‘Ah, yes. Helene, from the flower shop, says she is always popping in to say hello and see how you are going,’ the Mayor continued. ‘And I hear she’s not the only one.’

The villagers had taken to Marie who, despite her youthful look and vivacious character, turned out also to be an excellent and discreet listener. The salon rapidly became a meeting place – especially with no café close by.

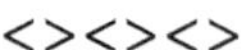

Six months down the track, *Top Coiff* started to show a reasonable profit. Despite being a busy salon, the villagers often called in for a chat with Marie, or with another of the clients.

‘I have another idea.’ Marie told Henri.

‘What’s that?’

‘Well, we can put the rest of the warehouse space to good use. We can have a small coffee corner to go with the salon. Perhaps add a few books and more magazines. Everyone in the village complains that there is nowhere close by to enjoy a coffee and a chat, and they keep calling in at the salon. It would be pleasant to have a few tables and chairs for them to relax in and catch up with each other – and it also means they won't stand around me while I'm cutting someone's hair.'

'Your mother is right. You don't stand still for long! But I like that,' Henri said. 'I'll look into what's needed.'

The salon continued to flourish, and the coffee corner became the favourite haunt for locals, with an increased flow of visitors. To begin with, a pot of coffee was made available for clients and visitors to help themselves, and an honour system was in place for people to leave a tip or gift to cover expenses. One of the clients also brought in some potted palms to fill the empty corners. Marie then added one of the old sofas from her bungalow to add warmth and character to the place.

The coffee corner's popularity helped increase salon trade to the extent that Marie had to take on another assistant. Henri volunteered to help as the barista, making the coffee in the modern coffee machine that Marie had insisted upon buying. 'It will be a change to be with all the women rather than all the men at the pub down the road,' he joked.

Marie had a knack of eliciting what her clients longed for or missed. As she took in her clients' concerns, aches and pains, and troubles, she unconsciously started to draw on her knowledge of herbal teas and remedies. Marie discovered she had the same innate knowledge of how to use herbs and tinctures, a trait she had obviously inherited from her aunt. Whenever she went to Sainte Anne to stock up her shop, she would drop into the herbal shop in town and pick up some teas and oils for particular clients. Sometimes she would also pick up a few special gifts.

When Henri came to pick her up, after one of her city excursions, he joked, 'At this rate, you might as well stock the salon with this stuff, Marie. On every visit, you buy more and more of it.'

'What a great idea! We can get a few shelves and stock them with herbal teas, remedies and oils – and perhaps a few gifts. I remember *Tante* Juliette's shop in Paris. It was always buzzing with people – just like the salon!'

'Oh no, you're off again. Silly me, giving you ideas. If you are going to expand, you must charge properly for the goods and services,'

Henri chided gently. 'You hardly turn a profit, and you still have a loan to repay. It's a good thing the salon is so busy!'

There was soon another addition to the coffee corner. Celine, one of Marie's regulars, sat down with Marie and Henri one afternoon.

'You know I make all sorts of pickled vegetables, fruit compotes, jams and other delicious produce. I sell them from the shed at the back of my home. You have such a large area here. Why don't I use the rest of the coffee corner?'

'Oh Celine, it's a lovely thought.' Marie looked confused and uncomfortable. Celine was a favourite client of hers, but Marie felt stretched to the limit. 'But...'

Before she could finish, Henri cut in. 'Marie hardly copes with the coffee corner and the herbal remedies as it is...'

'I thought that was the case. But I have a plan! I can look after the 'shop' – not just my produce, but your products too. And I can help with the café especially when you are not around Henri.'

Celine's involvement was a stroke of luck. She got along with Marie as the two developed a close friendship. She was a useful addition to the salon cum café, cum shop, helping whenever she could. This made it easier for Marie to spend time and interact with her clients.

As the villagers discovered that Marie had a penchant for giving practical advice, they confided in her more and more. Sometimes it was a case of putting people together. When Marie learnt that one of her elderly woman clients was finding living alone more difficult - and losing sleep about it, she decided to take the matter in hand. She introduced her elderly client to the daughter of one of the local fishermen. The daughter had just got married. The young couple were too hard up to rent a place of their own.

With Marie co-ordinating and helping set up the meetings, the two parties met at Marie's coffee shop to discuss how living together could work out for the benefit of both parties. The outcome was that the young couple moved in to the upstairs floor of the two-storey home where they could enjoy their privacy, leaving the bottom floor bedroom and bathroom to their benefactor, so she would not have to navigate stairs. In return, the young couple took over the housework and looked after the garden. They also helped with the shopping, and sometimes with the cooking.

Of course, whatever Marie was involved with became the next day's village gossip, especially with a helping hand from Celine who was Marie's greatest admirer.

'Ah Marie, that oil you suggested worked well. I followed your instructions and rubbed it onto my sore joints.' That feedback came from another of Marie's clients and referred to the wintergreen oil Marie had recommended.

'A cup of thyme tea after dinner is doing wonders to my digestion,' crooned another satisfied client.

'Bonjour Marie,' Bridgette greeted her on one of her regular visits. 'I have looked into your suggestion of doing up the park outside the council office. The villagers are keen on your idea of a community centre near the park that can be used for special occasions such as weddings, and can also be used as a meeting place for different groups and perhaps to host a village fête.'

'That's good news. I'm happy to hear that,' Marie replied, as she snipped away at the Mayor's hair. 'We should have more activities to keep our senior citizens engaged. And a centre in the middle of the village would be accessible to most people,' Marie replied. 'But you're not your usual bubbly self. Is anything the matter, Madame *Maire*?'

'You are so intuitive, Marie,' the Mayor replied. 'I have a headache coming on.'

'I have just the remedy for you.' Marie walked over to where she kept the essential oils and selected a small bottle of lavender oil. 'Rub this gently onto your temple,' Marie advised.

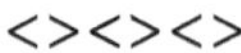

Bridgette called into the salon on a Friday morning for her usual hair wash and set. Unusually that morning, Marie was on the phone. She looked rather worried, which was also very curious. The Mayor took a seat – a little bit closer to Marie, as she could not resist the temptation to overhear what the call was about.

'Oh *Maman*! You should have called immediately and told me what was happening,' the Mayor heard Marie say.

'Is everything all right?' a concerned Bridgette asked Marie when she got off the phone.

'Yes...yes,' came the distracted response.

When Marie got home that evening morning, she told her uncle about her conversation with her mother.

'It is so unusual for *Maman* to call,' Marie started out. 'So I knew immediately something was wrong. Then she tells me that she had fallen, hurt her back, and broken her leg. I speak with her every day, yet she never said a word before now.'

'Amélie can be like that,' Henri replied, shaking his head.

'It has not healed well and is causing much pain. *Maman* has to give up her Paris apartment. That is certain. The stairs are too much for her.'

"That's not good at all.'

'I've been thinking about it all day. I am going to suggest that she joins me here, in Guadeloupe.'

'It will be hard on her, moving away from friends and the life she knew. You had better see what she wants to do.'

'You are right. We will have to ask *Maman.* It's her decision. I can move into the bungalow so I can help look after her,' Marie continued. 'It means less income, but the salon is doing well and we will manage.'

Later that evening Marie called her mother and they had a good, long chat.

'Are you sure you can accommodate me? I do not wish to be a burden to you.' Amélie said. 'If I have to move from my apartment, away from my friends, I may as well move to Guadeloupe. I loved growing up there, and I will be with you and Henri.'

'It will be so lovely to be together again! How much time do you need to get ready?'

'Let me speak to *Tante* Juliette. She has offered me her spare room until I decide what to do. And she will help me with moving and whatever is necessary.'

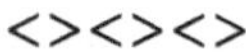

The next morning Marie asked Celine to rearrange her appointments so that she had time to go to Sainte Anne. Marie's first stop was the travel agency to look into what it would entail to fly someone over who had mobility problems. She was shocked to discover that her mother would probably need a business class ticket where she could put her leg up, as it would be too painful to sit through the nine-hour flight. She would also need someone to accompany her to get to the airport, and on and off the planes.

Marie's absence from the salon was a bonus to Bridgette. She found Henri and Celine in the coffee corner of the salon and sat down for a lengthy chat.

'What's going on Henri?' the Mayor asked.

Henri knew it was pointless to resist. He recounted all that his niece had told him. 'Amélie has decided to take up Marie's offer and come and live here with her. In fact, she went into the city today to find out about flights and getting her mother here. Amélie can't walk well yet, and it's a long flight.'

'We must help her,' Bridgette replied, without hesitation.

'What do you have in mind?'

'I'm not sure yet, but keep me informed.'

'We don't have much time.'

'Then I had better start straight away.'

The village had never seen Bridgette so full of drive and determination. Suddenly, the Mayor was flitting in and out of shops and offices, and busily chatting away with several people.

When Marie returned to the village, she immediately went to the salon to tell Henri about her plans.

'The air ticket is expensive. *Maman* will have to fly business class. She will probably need someone with her to manage the luggage and help her along the way. That's all going to be costly. Tomorrow I will make an appointment with Michel, the bank manager, to ask about a small loan.'

'I wish I could help,' Henri continued.

'You have been a great help already. A small loan from the bank should not be a problem.'

The following morning Henri was impatient to get out of his home to go and update Bridgette.

'It is as I suspected,' Bridgette replied. 'Leave it with me Henri.' She had guessed well – there was a financial issue. With that, she got up, swung her large handbag on her shoulder, and hurried off, leaving a puzzled Henri wondering what she was up to.

Two days later Marie called in to see her bank manager at the appointed time.

'Is anything wrong, Marie?' queried Michel, seeing her unusually troubled face. Michel had become a good friend, giving sound advice on how to run a small business.

'Yes and no,' she replied. 'It's my mum. She lives in Paris in an apartment but she fell and broke her leg.' Marie explained the situation.

'So how can we help?' Michel asked.

'I need a small loan to cover the airfares. I still have to find someone to accompany her, and if necessary I will ask Henri to go and help her come over.'

'Let's see,' Michel replied, pulling up the relevant files on his computer screen. 'Your business is doing well and your repayments are up-to-date. The rental income from the bungalow has helped reduce the loan significantly. I can organise a small overdraft, but if we can add it to the loan, seeing how you are ahead, you will get a better interest rate. How urgent is this? I may need a few days.'

'Ah, if you must!' a disappointed Marie exclaimed. She had wanted an immediate answer. 'Well, I still have to hear from *Maman* about when she is ready to come over. It would be reassuring to know that I can afford to do so.'

'Please don't worry. We will definitely help you out. Just give me a little leeway.' Michel squirmed in his seat uncomfortably. What Michel did not tell Marie was that his aunt, the Mayor, had phoned to explain the situation. Waving aside his concerns about interference with clients, she had asked him to defer any decision about a loan for a day or two until she put her own plan into action.

Bridgette had been busy in other ways. That same day, she met with Henri at her office, laid out her plan, and instructed him on what to do. 'We meet here again tomorrow morning, to make the final arrangements.'

'Marie went to the bank today to ask for a loan,' Henri warned.

'Not to worry... it's all in hand,' the Mayor gave an enigmatic smile.

Bridgette waved excitedly when Henri called in, the next day. 'It's all in place,' she stated proudly. 'Have you spoken to Amélie again? Has she confirmed our plans?'

'Yes, she has, Madame *Maire*,' Henri replied, smiling broadly. 'How can we ever thank you?'

The Mayor waved the gratitude away. 'The next step is as we had discussed. Tell Marie that you have arranged for her to visit the aged care facility in the village in case her mother will need full time care. We have to get her there at all costs. If she hesitates, then you must insist that it is a prudent step for her to take to ensure she is able to understand what taking on her mother entails.' The Mayor winked at Henri conspiratorially. 'I will confirm the date and time. Then Celine can inform the rest of the community.'

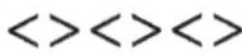

'*Maman* says that she will be able to tell me when she is ready to fly over in a few days,' Marie told Henri one evening, a few days later. 'And Michel had confirmed the loan. He advised me to give him a day's warning before taking out the money.'

'You know what banks are like – all the paperwork! He's a good man.'

'And are you still happy to fly over and accompany *Maman* here?

'But of course!' Henri paused, and then added, 'By the way, do not forget tomorrow's appointment with the nursing hostel manager. We have to be there at 11.00am.'

'I asked Celine to contact my appointments and reschedule. She will look after the clients.' Marie paused, and then continued 'Do we have to go?'

'Yes. I think it is important to be aware of all the aspects that looking after Amélie will entail.'

<><><>

Marie walked into the nursing hostel, followed by an excited and nervous Henri.

'What's up?' she asked him, looking back. 'You are not your usual calm self.'

Henri held open the door, and Marie entered. As she turned her head to view the lobby, she was surprised to see banners and balloons hanging around the place. She was even more surprised as her eyes first landed on Bridgette and then on the older woman in a wheel chair beside her. She shook herself and looked again.

Amélie smiled back at her. 'What wonderful friends you have, my dear,' she said, opening her arms for a big hug with her daughter. Next to her mum stood Catherine, an airhostess, and one of Marie's clients. She had obviously accompanied her mother.

'But ..but how???' Marie stammered.

'Your vitality and enthusiasm, and your ideas for improving the village have brought us closer together. You are one of us,' Bridgette replied, a broad smile on her face, as many of Marie's clients looked on. 'And we look after our own.'

Then the Mayor turned to Marie's mother. 'Welcome home, Amélie. You have a beautiful daughter!'

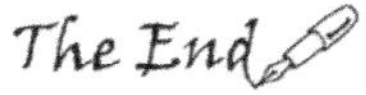

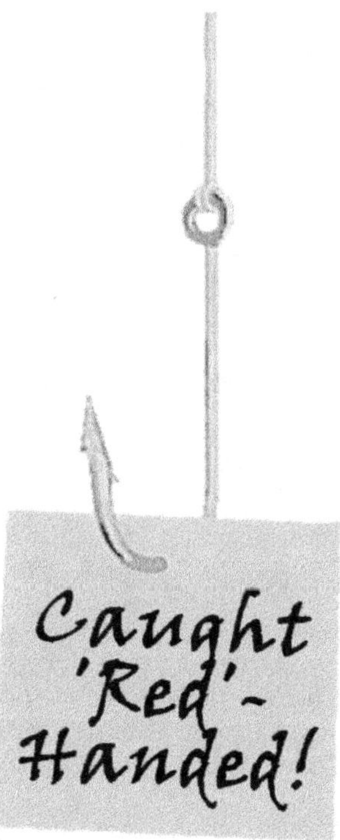
Caught
'Red'-
Handed!

The Rummy Game:

For the uninitiated, the rummy group in this short story played with two decks of cards consisting of the four suits: two black suits - spades (♠) and clubs (♣) and two red suits - hearts (♥) and diamonds (♦). Players put down a twenty-point counter for each game, and placed a ten-point counter as a side bet. They could 'buy' up to four times during play and each buy cost another five points.

Ten cards were then dealt to each player, and if anyone had the same card as the first upturned card, they won the ten point counter pot.

At the end of each game, the winner won the twenty point counter pot, which also included the counters from any of the players' buys. The counters were then converted to points that went towards the total quarterly tally to reveal the overall winner.

It had been Angie's idea: a Rummy group that would meet weekly. The original group had consisted of Angie, Kath and Stephanie, Steffie to her friends. The three women had met at the local primary school where their children had started out on their school years.

Angie and Kath lived in the same street in Attadale, Western Australia, and their two daughters, Clare and Anna, were inseparable. Steffie's son, Nick, was a frequent visitor to the girls' homes.

Stuart, Angie's brother, joined the rummy group along the way. To keep him company, Steffie's husband Greg also joined up, thus making it a group of five.

Such was the bond that had developed with all the players that they sometimes travelled together on holidays, with their partners and children in tow. The group had watched each other's children grow up, looking out for them, especially through their children's turbulent teenage years. They were a cheerful, warm-hearted group, generous and sociable.

At the children gained more independence, so did the adults. Their weekly get-together shifted from evenings, to after work hours. Then as the retirement years loomed, this morphed into leisurely afternoons, sometimes well into the evening. The group migrated from one of their houses to the tranquil Point Walter reserve: a natural wooded area with adjoining park and sandbar that jutted out into the middle of the Swan River.

It was an idyllic life. Cards, coffee, then a glass of wine or two... and maybe some nibbles or the occasional dinner at the local café - this became the norm on Thursdays. Steffie and Greg, the only couple who still worked, arranged their diaries to fit around this, lapping up the relaxed entertainment that the afternoons in the scenic reserve offered.

Then, after thirty years of playing cards amicably, it all started to come undone!

The trouble began when Angie introduced a change to the rummy game. 'The other rummy group I play with have added a bit of wagering spice to playing. They use twenty and fifty cent penalties during various stages of playing.'

'Oh that could be fun!' Greg offered.

'I don't like the idea of using coins,' Steffie pointed out. 'They're messy and we have to carry them around.

'We can use counters instead!' Stuart suggested.

'Great idea. I like that,' Steffie said. 'We can put in a number of counters for each round we play. That way, the game becomes more interesting.'

'At present, we play a number of rounds until one of us wins the overall game. How will the wagering work? Does the game change at all?' Kath asked.

'Not really,' Angie explained. 'The losers of

each round give their card tally as usual.' This meant that each player added up any cards remaining in their hand according to the face value of each card, with the Jack, Queen, and King, the court or face cards, attracting a penalty of 10 points each. There were two Jokers available and each one attracted a twenty-five point penalty.

'I will still record the points for each player as usual,' Angie continued. In the game, if the number of points for each round exceeded a hundred, a star was marked against the player's name, with an appropriate penalty. A player won the full rummy game when all other players' cards added to over a hundred.

'Why don't Angie and I work out a counter handicap?' Stuart suggested. 'We can then take it from there.'

The revised version of the rummy game was an immediate winner with the group. It introduced an on-going, competitive element, and everyone played with gusto.

At the end of each quarter, Angie tallied the points.

'I'm sure I'm ahead,' Stuart started out.

Everyone eagerly following the process. In real terms, the stakes were paltry. However, each player scrutinised the proceedings so closely that a casual observer could easily have jumped to the conclusion that the winnings were substantial.

'Steffie is the overall winner! She has won the greatest number of points.'

'I'm sure I was ahead,' broke out Stuart excitedly. 'Let's check again.' A recheck of the tally showed that Stuart was about forty points short, much to his dismay.

'We now have to choose a restaurant to celebrate the end of the quarter.' Greg said.

'Yes, and Steffie only gets to pay ten percent of her bill. The rest of us pay according our ranking,' continued Angie.

'Kath is running late today,' Angie started out. It was a balmy autumn afternoon, and Angie was watching the black swans that inhabited the area glide by.

'Hmm, ...Kath,' Greg mused.

'What about Kath?' Steffie asked.

'I think she's cheating.'

'Yes, I think so too,' Angie broke in. 'Oh hell! I hoped I was wrong. Our girls are best friends. After all these years, this is a difficult one to handle It's been troubling me for some time. What can we do about it?'

'We all know she hates losing. Yet, we can't confront her. It will destroy the group.' Stuart said.

"There's no way I will rock the boat by saying anything,' Steffie continued.

'Sometimes people are caught shoplifting. They can't help it, even though they can well afford to buy the products. I think it's called kleptomania,' Greg volunteered. 'Maybe Kath has some such illness.'

Unable to figure out how to handle the delicate situation, nothing was said or done to begin with. Angie, Steffie, Stuart and Greg hoped Kath would change her ways.

It soon became difficult to tolerate the cheating, especially when sometimes it was blatant. Before long, snide comments were starting to infiltrate the card game.

The next time the rummy party met, Stuart attempted to deal with the problem directly. 'Perhaps it's a good idea if we can all place our cards face up on the table after each game. Then Angie has more time to record everyone's points.'

It was to no avail. Kath ignored the suggestion with the comment: 'Oh, I always remember my card tally.' Kath had a way of sneaking in her cards with the rest of the deck on the table, so that it was impossible to check them. Calling her out was out of the question.

One time Angie, who was sitting next to Kath, caught sight of Kath's cards as she put them down, claiming 57 points. A gust of wind blew them, overturning some of the cards, enough to reveal several face cards that showed that Kath's tally could not have been correct. Though Kath reacted quickly to cover the cards, Stuart could see that they very obviously amounted to more than she had declared.

Kath realised that Stuart had caught her out, but she stared him out and brazenly continued as if nothing had happened.

Angie caught Stuart's eye. Both were now sure that Kath was cheating. It irked them immensely, especially as they felt so helpless to take any action that would jeopardise the group's cohesion.

'I'm taking a comfort break,' announced Kath, as she got up. 'I'll be back in a jiffy!'

As soon as Kath left the table and was out of earshot, Stuart and Angie quickly related what they had just witnessed. The rest of the group broke into hot discussion.

"It's just not right! Or fair! I know it's only a game, but it bothers me that she can do this to us!' Angie said.

'It has certainly cast a shadow on our fun Thursdays. Again, what can we do?

The issue was eating away at the rest of the group. At their wit's end, they explored options.

'I feel helpless and angry. She knows, and yet she persists. Maybe Greg is right. It is a sickness of some type. But if so, how can we help her?' Steffie said.

'It can't be one of us that confronts her. It will simply destroy our friendship.' That was from Stuart.

“And that’s too high a price to pay for a card game!’ Angie concluded.

The game resumed, yet the group were not their usual jovial selves. It was stalemate: they were unhappy with the situation but unable to find a way forward.

Yet sometimes, when you are at your wits’ end, fate intervenes.

It was a mild wintry and sunny afternoon at Point Walter. The group had gathered for their usual Thursday entertainment. The reserve was popular that day, with families all around them enjoying the lovely balmy weather.

The card game was progressing as usual, and today it was Steffie’s turn to have a winning streak. All around, kids played on the beach, climbed trees or on the nearby play equipment. Among them were Kath’s grandchildren. Kath’s daughter had come down to catch up with her mother, enjoying the fresh air whilst her boys used up their excess energy.

‘I’m out,’ Steffie said triumphantly, presenting her winning hand of cards to the table.

‘Well done, Steff. Okay everyone give me your points.’

‘I’m gone. A star! I have over a hundred points.’ Greg said.

Kath called out, ‘53 for me’.

Kath’s ten-year-old grandson who had been standing behind her watching the game suddenly stepped forward and interrupted.

‘Gran!’ he called out. ‘That’s more than 53!’

Leaning forward he grabbed the cards out of his grandmother’s hands before she could gather her wits to react. He eagerly turned them over, spreading them on the table.

Poor Kath was stunned. Usually so cautious, she had been unaware of her grandson behind her.

There, in plain sight, was a ‘red’ suited hand: the King of Diamonds, and a set comprising the King, Queen and Jack of Hearts. Alongside them, grinning wickedly was the jolly Joker - already 55 points by anyone’s count!

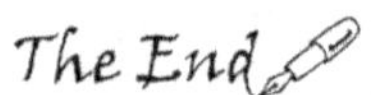

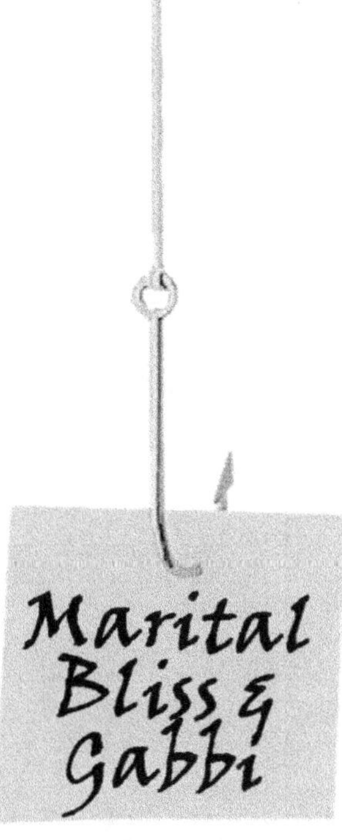
Marital
Bliss &
Gabbi

'Hmmm...'

Petra stirred. It was approaching that time of morning when she would have to drag herself out of bed.

She loved staying up late at night and chatting into the wee hours of the morning, but John would not have any of that. He was a definite morning person - a very early riser.

'Morning darling,' he grinned.

Through half-open eyes she caught sight of his mischievous gleam. Moreover, his intentions were readily manifest as he drew closer, letting the familiarity of years of bliss take over.

Petra was not too sure if she was awake or

dreaming. It was a pleasant sensation and she did not intend to put a stop to it. She felt her body slowly respond, as the layers of slumber slipped away - slowly, lovingly and tenderly. An awareness of self came over her.

'I love you', she whispered ...and then froze!

Petra looked at John and over his shoulder. Yes, once again Gabbi was up early, and on the prowl.

Gabriella, or Gabbi as they called her, was their delightful three-year-old, a most mischievous and talkative young lady.

'I come to keep you company,' she proffered, opening the door to their bedroom. Obviously, she had dragged along her teddy, her quilt cover, and half the contents of her bedroom.

'Today I woke up early because I have a lot of work to do,' Gabbi continued importantly.

'And daddy, we have to go to the deer park today because we haven't gone for a wery, wery long time.'

Gabbi still had problems pronouncing her 'v' and sometimes her 'r's.

She crawled onto the bed, as Petra and John gently extricated themselves, trying to hide their nakedness, or rather, their intentions.

'Yak, yak, yak ...just like her mum,' John whispered into Petra's ear.

'Look, it's only five' o'clock, darling. You will be tired for the rest of the day. Go on, back to your own bed. I'll come and get you with a big hug at seven.'

Petra fished about for her dressing gown, which she drew around her before slipping out of bed.

'I'll walk you back and tuck you in.' She winked at John. The look in her eyes spoke volumes.

Petra took her daughter by the hand, and guided her back to her bedroom.

'There you are darling. Here's teddy and Nyaree, and little clown. Now close your eyes and try to go back to sleep.'

'Yes mummy,' Gabbi replied as she screwed up her eyes, trying hard to obey.

Petra tiptoed back to the bedroom. 'I don't know if we are safe,' she whispered as she rejoined her husband in bed.

'Just come and lie down beside me.'

So lay Petra and John, as the advent of

daylight grew more pronounced. The minutes ticked by, quietly; no sound at all. It felt wonderfully luxurious to have a peaceful moment, just for the two of them. Once the day began, it was all rush, with constant demands on their time. They grew confident and felt reassured as they allowed their bodies to stir once more.

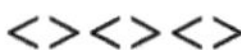

The bedroom door was suddenly thrown wide open, as Gabbi burst in. ‘I’m going to use your toilet,’ she announced. ‘I need to do wee wees.’

John and Petra just lay there, stunned. Gabbi walked past pulling up her pyjama top whilst simultaneously trying to push her pants down, and in this fashion, she wiggled her way to the bathroom. They listened to the unabashed sound effects of their three-year-old going through the motions, chatting all the while.

‘I’ve got an elephant soap and a fishy soap,’ Gabbi continued, ‘so I am going to wash my hands in my bathwoom.’

‘Yes dear,’ was all Petra could manage. Her little daughter usually slept in until 7.30am or even later. Yet Gabbi always seemed to know when mum and dad did not wish to be disturbed. It was like this in the evenings as well. No time was sacred any more.

'Then I'll go back to bed, because I must sleep a bit more. And daddy, tomowwow you must wead me a stowy. Yesterday,' she gasped for breath, 'yesterday, you didn't wead me one!'

'Yes darling - close the door, will you?'

Their bodies were still close; their emotions far too aroused to be ignored.

Like teenagers, John and Petra felt themselves steal at the precious minutes of intimacy, as quiet ruled over the household once again. There was an irresistible sense of mischief in having to grab surreptitiously at these moments of privacy. Gone were those lazy days of comfortable lovemaking 'on demand'. The children saw to that.

'I love you,' John started out. 'And I thought I was getting to be too old for a quickie', he grinned.

They just lay in cosy intimacy, enjoying the sounds of morning as they introduced the day: the creaking of the house as the sun warmed up the roof, the birds at that particular time of sunrise, and the automatic sprinklers whose whooshing sounds marked time.

'Mummy', Gabbi stormed in, full of importance, bursting into speech once more.

'You know its morning time. And I can't find my textas. Did Ryan hide them from me? ...I think I want to be near you mummy.'

Gabbi clambered onto the bed. Angie glanced sideways to see John cupping his hands over his nether regions for protection, as their daughter clumsily made her way over them, unaware of their groans as she sank feet, knees, and elbows into their bodies. It was never enough to climb into bed with them. She had to lie in the middle.

Aware of his wife's eyes on him twinkling with humour, John grimaced theatrically and then turned his gaze towards his rascally little daughter with pride.

'You are both pests,' he proclaimed. 'But I wouldn't have it any other way.'

The End

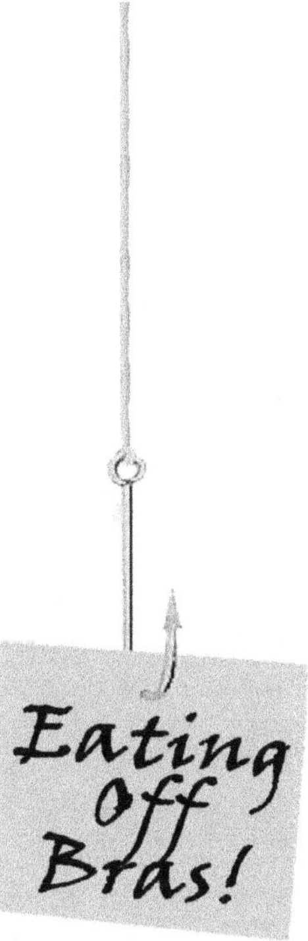
Eating
Off
Bras!

Prelude:

The author, Christina, and her husband Bjorn, both ocean-going yachties (yachting people), were sailing up the Red Sea in their yacht on their way from Australia to the Mediterranean. In a large bay south of Egypt, they ran into some strong winds and had to take shelter in an anchorage called Ras Banas. Two other boats made it to the anchorage with them: another Australian couple lived on one of the boats, which they were sailing around the world, and the other boat was sailed solo by a Spaniard, accompanied by his dog.

The Spaniard was on his last leg of a circumnavigation, having departed from Spain, crossed the Atlantic to the Caribbean and to America. Then he had set off across the Pacific - which is where this story takes place. After the Pacific, the Spaniard continued on his journey around south-east Asia and across the Indian Ocean. Christina and Bjorn first met him when they were sailing up the Red Sea.

Ras Banas lies at the south-eastern tip of Egypt and on the border with Sudan. However, it is disputed territory, and at that time, it was guarded by the Egyptian armed forces. It was a No-Go zone and visitors were prohibited from being in the area. Boats are allowed to seek shelter but not to go ashore.

After three days cooped up on their boats, the sailors on the three boats were dying to go ashore and stretch their legs. The weather forecast showed the winds finally dying down. Communicating via VHF radio, the sailors decided to risk it and take a short stroll, especially to see the state of the sea after the storm and to ensure it was safe to leave the bay where they were anchored. They were eager to resume their journey northwards.

The five adults and dog made their way along the shore to the point to see if the swell was abating. It was about a thirty-minute walk. As they approached, a young Egyptian soldier sprung up in front of them, seemingly out of nowhere and challenged the group.

'No tourist here. NO!' the guard shouted, waving his menacing rifle wildly, and then pointing it ominously at them.

Joe, from the other Australian yacht, spoke gently explaining that they just wanted to stretch their legs.

The guard would have none of it. He broke into a tirade in Arabic, waving his gun and growing angrier by the minute. Christina, Maltese by birth, recognised some of the words, and picked up – in the growing fury of the soldier - his outrage and frustration, especially as none of the group could speak Arabic.

'Go on, Chris. Speak to him in Maltese,' Bjorn suggested.

Christina proceeded to speak slowly and gently in Maltese, which is a Semitic based language (and written with a Latin script). She explained that they wanted to ascertain that the sea conditions had died down enough for the group to sail away. She said that they would return to their boats immediately.

The effect was instantaneous. The soldier seemed to understand the author, even if it was not quite his type of Arabic. He gaped at the group incredulously and the gun slowly came down.

'Morru, morru!' he ordered, waving the group back to the boats.

The group needed no urging to hurry back, practically walking on water.

'I need a stiff drink after that,' the author said, looking back surreptitiously to check that they were clear of the angry soldier and his gun.

'My boat is closest,' the Spaniard said. 'Let's all have a drink on board.'

And the story takes off from here.

PS: For more on the sailing trip from Australia to the Mediterranean, see the author's book: 'A Little Bit of MisChief.'

Eating off bras? ...No – not a titillating tale!

'I've got some good whisky on board,' Luis, the Spaniard offered.

'Yes please,' came the chorus. Four of us, two couples from two boats had joined Luis for a well-deserved stiff drink after the harrowing encounter with the fuming Egyptian soldier.

'He was so angry,' Joe, the sailor in the other boat said. 'But we were foolish to disregard the prohibition zone.'

'I thought that the place was deserted,' Christina explained. 'I haven't seen any sign of life on shore since we arrived, three days ago.'

As the group slowly started to breathe

regularly again, Christina turned to Luis. 'Did you say that you have sailed all the way round the oceans on your own?' she asked.

'Yes, except for Columbus, my dog. He's a better sailor than I am.' Luis was in his mid-thirties. His thirty-five foot boat looked like it had weathered many adventures, but was nevertheless well equipped and sound.

'How long have you been sailing? And, if you don't mind my asking, how do you fund the trip? Most of the round-the-world sailors are retirees, like us. But now and again you come across younger people who take up the challenge.' Bjorn asked.

'That's true,' Jim said. 'Remember the young Danish couple on the boat *Njord*? They had established a website that advertised round-the-world sailing holidays. They had two to four people sailing with them most of the time, and this paid their way across the oceans.'

'This is my fifth year, Luis countered. 'I had to take time off sailing now and again to earn enough money to keep going - and sometimes it was a challenge.

'To begin with, I sailed from Spain to the

Caribbean. It was easy to get work there. I did some diving on boats to clean the hulls to earn money. But I also used the time to speak to as many round-the-world sailors as possible to learn about the different destinations.

'The longest passage is of course the Pacific, and provisions are expensive on these islands. I had to come up with something that would help earn some money. Diving jobs would not pay the way, especially as so many of the Pacific islanders are such good divers.'

'So what did you do?'

'In Florida, I met a couple from Alaska. They had just completed their circumnavigation. "Everything is so expensive on those islands," Roy told me. He was referring in particular to French Polynesia. "Fruit and vegetables are scarce – and you had better not need any spares for the boat, as everything has to be flown in at great expense."'

Luis paused to have another sip of his scotch. Then he resumed his tale. 'It was his wife Judy who gave me the idea. She mentioned that Polynesian women often remarked at how thin she was. "At one stage, one of the women in the group prodded my arms. "All bone!" she told

Judy. Then the woman unexpectedly reached out and groped her boobs to see if she wore a bra. Judy was tall and thin – and almost flat chested!

'Not deterred, the Polynesian woman asked Judy if she had any spare brassieres – large sizes, that is. Then she asked about what clothes they carried on board their boat. When Judy questioned her interest, the woman explained that undergarments and the like were simply not available for sale on the islands.'

'Well, I thought about what Judy had said. The next day I approached her again. I asked her to give me more information about what the women wore and what they sought, or craved for. "Oh, all sorts of things... bras in particular... and they all seem to have enormous bosoms!"'

'I knew I had the answer.

'I spent the next three months in Miami working as a deck hand on a super yacht. Whilst there I visited as many Op shops as possible.' Op shops were second hand shops often run by various charities. 'I bought every brassiere – especially the larger sizes – I could lay my hands on. You should have seen the funny looks I got from some of the ladies running these places!'

'You sold bras in Polynesia?' Christina queried.

'Not quite. In the Marquesas, the first group of islands you sail to from the west coast of America, I went ashore with a box of assorted bras. There was some interest, but not as much as I had hoped for.'

Luis looked around at the sailors in the boat's cockpit, who were practically hanging on every word. He smiled.

'On my second day ashore, my luck changed. One of the local women strode up and looked into the box with interest. I quickly tried to figure out how much to charge for each bra, but my first client resolved the question. She rummaged around, selected two brassieres that she thought was her size, and then looked me in the eye.

'"I'll have these. You come for dinner tonight with my family, yes?"

'I jumped at the opportunity. Not only was I getting supplies, but I was also being fed. I had great seafood that evening, and my generous host even gave me a few provisions, explaining how to make use of local produce. The take-away bag she gave me included two types of bananas, one of which could be eaten raw and a second variety, *meia*, which had to be cooked before eating. She had also included some breadfruit, which she said was delicious when mashed with garlic and oil. Luckily, I had gone prepared with a spare bra, and handed this over in appreciation.

'The next day, more women came looking for bras. The challenge now was to restrict sales to the number of meals required, but on the first islands this kind of sorted itself out –some days I had breakfast, lunch and dinner, as well as a few provisions, as I could not get myself to refuse anyone a bra.'

'It seems like the first woman was the spokesperson for the islanders,' Joe's wife suggested.

'Yes I think so. It was the same on many of the other islands. One woman would come to inspect the box and then others would follow suit. Before long, the trading would start,' Luis stated.

'And did you manage to get fed every day?' Christina asked.

'Whilst at anchor on the islands, I found that was mostly the case. Of course, as you know, some of the anchorages are uninhabited. Also, there can be passages of up to a week between the groups of Pacific Islands. With planning, I could ask for produce instead of a meal in exchange for the bras.' Luis paused, sipping his scotch.

'I never really had to purchase any food. And of course, I always put out a line when I was sailing. The fishing was quite good, and kept me going in more isolated atolls and islands.'

Luis paused once again, and a big smile spread on his face. You could see his punch line coming up.

'I knew that I had chosen well in stocking up with the brassieres when I got to one of the smaller islands in Polynesia. By this stage, word had spread that I had bras for trading. Sometimes I would be met with a canoe-load of women wanting to inspect my wares.

'The most enduring memory was when I went ashore on one particular island, after a very warm welcome and several bra trades. As I strolled down what represented the main street, three women, wearing their traditional colourful clothing walked towards me. They were wearing one of my bras on the outside of their tops! They waved cheerfully, with a welcoming smile. The bras had become the local status symbol.'

'That's amazing – and very clever of you!' Joe said.

Then Luis raided his whisky glass in salute, and continued, '...And that was how I funded the provisioning for the passage across the Pacific Ocean – eating off bras.'

The End

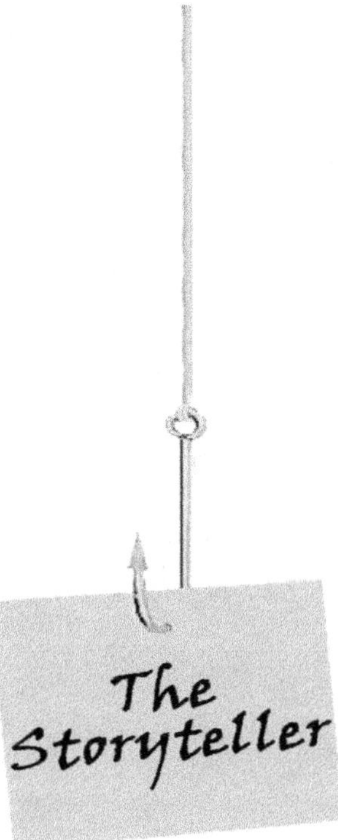
The
Storyteller

'Hello!' a voice called out.

Camille was trying to fix the engine again. The 2-cylinder marine diesel on her sailing boat had a mind of its own and needed constant attention. 'Bloody engine!' she swore.

Camille had heard the greeting - not a voice she recognised. Standing in the open cockpit of her boat, head down in the bilges, and grease over her hands and probably her face, she ignored the call and cursed the stubborn engine instead.

'Hello, can I help?'

A male voice - and it sounded uncomfortably close! Camille was mindful of her predicament.

If her head was in the bilge, all that presented out of the boat was her bikini-clad bum in the air. She was intrigued. Her boat was moored at the old Torpedo Depot in Msida Creek, a safe harbour - and usually a quiet place off the beaten track - on the island of Malta. She knew everyone along the small jetty. No passers-by came here.

Camille shrugged. Nothing she could do about it. She raised her head to see who was addressing her. A handsome man, probably in his sixties, looked down inquisitively at her from the neighbouring boat. She took in his smart blue pants and shirt, together with a cravat. She certainly did not miss his cheeky grin.

'It's the starter motor again. Probably needs changing.' Camille was determined not to show any embarrassment. 'Emm ...haven't seen you here before. Do you own the boat? Nobody's been on it for ages. By the way, I'm Camille.'

'I'm Alex. I bought the boat a year ago, but I've been away for a few months – health problems. ...It seems that the engine is giving you trouble.' Alex had a warm, welcoming smile. 'I just boiled the kettle. Why don't you come over for a nice cup of tea and tell me about your problem. I used to be a mechanic. Perhaps I can help.'

It was not the most promising start to what would become a lifelong friendship.

Alexei Suharov, known to his friends as Alex, had come to settle in Malta from England for his retirement. Camille, in her late teens, found Alex intriguing. He was knowledgeable and helpful, with a cheeky smile always lurking in the background. He was also quite a character who had lived a fascinating life.

With their boats berthed alongside, Camille and Alex were often to be found chatting about all sorts of technical issues related with boats and sailing. 'Why don't you come over for dinner tomorrow,' Alex started out. 'You can meet my wife Eva. And we will have a few other sailing friends over as well.'

'I'd love to,' Camille replied. Their shared love of sailing, had cemented their friendship, despite the age difference. Eva joined them on many of the sailing outings, often bringing along a wonderful array of nibbles and food, and the three of them enjoyed a number of sailing adventures together.

The couple became an important part of Camille's life. When Camille met Peter, he was introduced to Alex and Eva and soon became an integral part of the sailing circle. Peter and Alex got on like a house on fire, to the extent that Peter asked Alex to be his best man at his and Camille's wedding.

Camille and Peter travelled the world for a few years as Peter's work took him to all corners of the globe.

'How about a trip to Australia?' Camille asked Peter. 'I've just got a letter from Maggie.' Maggie was one of Camille's closest friends. 'She says it's an amazing country. She has settled in Perth and has invited us over.'

'Great idea! And Maggie is such fun,' Peter replied.

The impromptu visit to Western Australia changed everything. Camille and Peter fell in love with the country, took the plunge, and decided to settle down in Perth. They had hardly been there a year when Camille received a letter from Alex and Eva.

'Pete, you won't believe this! Guess who is coming to join us here? I'm so excited!'

'Who?' Peter asked, grabbing hold of the letter Camille was reading. 'Goodness, they're arriving in a month's time. Of course we must ask them to stay until they find their own place.'

Camille collected Alex and Eva at the airport. Camille enjoyed taking her dear friends around, as they looked for a house to live in. She was a little bit disappointed when they chose to live at the other end of the city. However, this was no deterrent to their friendship.

The two couples had always been close, so it was a natural progression for Alex and Eva to take on the role of adopted parents to the younger ones. With their gentle and wise, yet humorous ways, Alex and Eva helped Camille and Peter navigate the ups-and-downs of life and careers. Eventually, however, age turned the tables round. Camille in particular took on the role of carer, looking after them as they became elderly. The situation became acute when Alex lost his soul mate. Eva became ill, then passed away.

<><><>

'How are you this evening?' Camille greeted Alex when she called on him after work. Alex was now in his nineties, shortish after having shrunk due to a tough and hard life. This had left him with endless back problems and a bent-over posture. Age had simply accelerated that process. Despite the stoop, he was still distinguished looking, and always immaculately turned out.

'Missing Eva,' Alex started out, dressed in his smoking jacket, and pipe in hand. And of course, he wore a cravat, as always. 'But now that you are here, I'm feeling so much better. It's good of you to come and visit.'

Camille had a busy working life running a small, not-for-profit organisation. For the first few months after Eva had passed away, she called on Alex almost twice weekly. On weekends, Peter accompanied her, and they usually enjoyed a meal and a glass of wine at one of the local pubs.

'I'll see you on Wednesday evening,' Camille told Alex after one of their weekend visits.

Alex looked crestfallen. He had become used to the twice-weekly visits.

Camille took in his disappointed look. 'It's a long drive and I can only manage one midweek trip,' she said, half-apologetically, giving Alex a hug.

Alex had always been an accomplished raconteur. Despite his age, his mind was as active and alert as ever, and Camille's visits suddenly took on a new twist.

Alex embarked on his life story. He seemed to have a bottomless pit of tales to draw on, many that Camille had not heard before. Every time Camille went to visit, it increasingly became a challenge to leave. The stories were so interesting – and they kept coming.

'My father was a Naval Admiral. He was a Baron, and a distant relative to the Russian royal family,' Alex started out on one of Camille's visits. He was adept at eliciting fascinating insights into his early life, told in enticing instalments. Over the course of a few weeks, Alex related how his family had fled to Europe in the early 1920s in the aftermath of the Russian Revolution. Unfortunately, it had resulted in the end of his parents' marriage. His father established himself in Paris, whereas his mother, British by birth, returned to live in London, taking the children with her.

'So you went from your mansion in St Petersburg to live close to poverty in an orphanage in London,' Camille was awed.

'It was unsettling,' Alex elaborated. 'In those early teenage years, my father would suddenly summon me to Paris. I then found myself among well-heeled Russian émigrés trying to maintain their pre-revolutionary Russian culture and way of life.'

This was the stuff of fairy tales.

Camille and Peter had enjoyed several anecdotes of his fascinating life and experiences, but on one of their weekend visits, they discovered that Alex had served on a British naval training ship.

'My father was a Russian naval admiral and he knew many of his British counterparts. He arranged for me to join the British navy under command of a colleague. Oh, it was a horrible life! Conditions were harsh, almost inhumane and the unmitigated cruelty was endless. Then one day I just lost my temper and struck an officer. That was it! I jumped ship in Australia.'

'I remember you telling me that you had been to Western Australia before,' Camille broke in. 'You were felling trees? How did that come about?'

Over several glasses of wine and scotch, Alex continued to weave his web of life stories.

'I found work hewing trees and cutting timber in a desolate area close to Wave Rock in Western Australia. That was how I ruined my back.'

'So how did you end up back in England?' Camille asked, settling back in her chair.

Alex did not need much prompting, and was about to elaborate. Peter, however, had another view. Always a pragmatist and aware of the late hour, he intervened. 'That's for the next instalment,' he insisted.

Over the ensuing visits, the stories kept coming.

'When my father heard that I was living in isolation in the Australian wilderness, he ordered me back to Paris. He insisted I spend time with some friends of his in Sydney. He wanted to make sure that I had not adopted swearing and other vulgar language. He wanted to make sure that I was presentable.' Alex smiled, giving his most wicked grin. He took every opportunity to deviate into endless anecdotes of interactions with bush cutters and rangers, and of life in the Australian outback towns.

'After spending time with my father, I knew that I needed to build a life. So I moved back to England. I did anything and everything that came my way. I served petrol at one garage,' Alex paused to replenish the tobacco in his pipe, light it, then continue. 'I must tell you about the man I worked for there – not a nice man,' and off he went on another tangent, and yet another story.

Another time Alex spoke of his dear wife. 'Eva was my greatest asset and the turning point in my my life. She was a Russian émigré herself. Her parents fled the revolution and settled in the east end of London. Her father was a jeweller. Ah,' Alex paused in reflection. 'Eva was an accomplished violinist and singer. I met her on the pier at Brighton one evening, where she was performing. I heard her singing and I was enchanted - and smitten! Well, that was the start of a loving, life-long relationship.'

It was time to replenish his pipe, which was never far from his reach.

'Eva's father disapproved of me,' Alex continued. 'I had to work very hard to earn his trust. But Eva was adamant. She stood firm, and he slowly relented. It helped that I had been building aircraft engines.'

'Building aircraft engines?' Peter was intrigued by this tantalising twist. This time it was his turn to be drawn in. 'How did that happen? You worked on an assembly line?'

'Oh no! We did it all by hand. We built our own tools, and then crafted each part of the engine individually.'

'How did you land a job like that? Did you have any engineering experience?' Peter asked, ever the pragmatic one.

'Well, I had had several casual jobs, usually working on and around cars, and then I started working on the engines. Then this job came up with Bristol aircraft. I spent the better part of the Second World War working on aircraft engines. It was vital to the War effort.'

'What aircraft?' Peter was fascinated.

'They were *Beaufighter* long-range planes...'

'And this impressed Eva's dad?' Camille asked, trying to get back to the main story.

'Well, my training in precision engineering helped and he took me under his wing. I learnt the trade and became a watchmaker and jeweller. Then with Eva's help we opened a jewellery and watch shop in south-east London.'

'So you settled down there?' asked Camille.

'Yes, the business prospered and we had a good time. I have always loved motor cars, especially fast cars. My favourite was the Riley Sports Special. Eva and I had some marvellous holidays driving on the continent, especially around Spain, Italy, and France.'

Alex had a minor car accident when he was about ninety-two. He hesitated when crossing a main road, and ended up sideswiped by an oncoming car. He realised that his reactions had slowed down significantly and, reluctantly, gave up driving. Without his few outings, he became more house bound and grew lonely.

This was when he changed tactics once more, and his almost daily phone conversations with Camille took on yet another twist.

It started one late morning, well timed just before the lunch break, when Camille's private cell phone rang. 'Hello Alex? How are you today?'

'Oh, I had a bad night, and I am feeling a bit weak and faint. Do you think you could come and visit? This could be it, you know...' his faint voice trailing off.

Camille grabbed her jacket and car keys. 'Family emergency!' she called out as she rushed past her secretary.

It took a good hour for Camille to drive to Alex's house in the northern suburbs of Perth. Throughout the journey, her mind kept on wandering on what she would find when she got there. She had a spare key to his house, just in case, but knocked loudly when she arrived to ensure he would hear her.

Alex opened the door calmly and ushered Camille inside. 'I have a lovely cup of tea for you,' he greeted her, eyes twinkling, pipe in hand and in his smoking jacket as usual.

Camille could not believe her eyes! Where was the weak, gasping man at death's doorstep that she had been so worried to find?

'And perhaps a touch of whisky?' he added, mischievously.

'Whisky? It's 12.30pm!' Camille protested. Then she reflected. 'Hmm... You certainly seem and sound better than you did when you called. I didn't know what to expect.' She heaved a big sigh of relief and continued, 'But I'm glad you're feeling better.'

Alex quickly looked away. Camille was sure that she caught a slight grin.

Alex prepared a cup of tea and brought out some freshly made ham and tomato sandwiches. 'You must be hungry,' he smiled innocently. He sat down in his favourite armchair, asked how Camille was. Then he started out on one of his stories as though this was just another normal visit.

Camille was so stunned that she just sat and listened.

'Do you remember when we sailed to the island of Gozo and your dad was on board.' Gozo is the sister island to Malta. 'It was very windy, and the anchor was dragging. And your dad told me to give him the spare anchor. Ah, those were the days... what lovely memories I have of your family. I do miss them.'

Before Camille could put a word in, Alex continued. 'Your dad wanted to swim out and drop the anchor further forward. I argued that he could not swim with a heavy anchor and chain. They would drag him down. Your dad shrugged away my concerns. He was very fit and a strong swimmer - and he proved me wrong.'

'Yes, I do remember,' Camille replied. Before she knew it, however, Alex was on to another anecdote and soon they were busy reminiscing on their sailing days around the island.

'Oh hell! It's two o'clock! I have to get back to the office – goodness I lost all track of time.'

Alex let Camille leave without protest. On the way back to the office, she had this feeling that somehow the whole visit had been a set-up by her astute adopted parent. Alex had succeeded in luring her into his den, so to speak, and then extending her visit, once again.

That evening, whilst cooking dinner, Camille told David about the call from Alex.

'I was so worried that I just dropped everything and left the office. And then when I got there, he was as right as rain.'

'You've been taken in,' Peter said, a broad smile on his face. 'But surely you realise he's been doing that for ages. Every time we visit, he always ends up relating his wonderful life stories - And in those unusual moments when he has run short of stories, he turns the conversation to politics because he knows you cannot resist!'

Peter looked Camille in the eye, then continued humorously, 'And don't complain, because when you two start discussing politics, there's no end to it. Alex revels in it, and so do you.'

'He's had such an interesting life, and always manages to come up with something new. And as to his politics, we're usually on the same page.'

'Alex called again this morning,' Camille told Peter over the phone, a few weeks later. 'He sounded weak and a bit depressed. I told him I would visit before coming home; make sure he is coping on his own. Can you join us?'

When Camille got to his house, Alex was practically waiting for her at the door.

'Here you are. A whisky is what you need after

the long drive.' Alex greeted Camille with a cheeky, bright smile on his face. 'And I asked Jim at the pub if he would deliver a nice rare rump steak with vegetables for dinner for three. I take it Peter is coming too?'

Camille shook her head in disbelief. Before she could say anything, Alex guided her to the dining room, which was all set up. 'The dinner should be here any minute now.'

Dinner and Peter arrived simultaneously and the three of them sat down to a tasty meal with a good bottle of red wine to wash it down. After dinner, Alex insisted on another whisky. Soon, he was in his stride again, relating some gripping episode from his life. He would tell his stories like an experienced angler, casting his lures, weaving, strategizing and changing topic to keep his young friends engaged ...until he had Camille, in particular, well and truly hooked.

That evening he started out with one of the stories of his life in a Russia still under the Tsar Nicholas.

'When I was around six years of age, I went missing for hours, and the whole household was out looking for me – both inside the mansion where we lived and in the surrounding forest.

There were bears around. In spring, they can be particularly dangerous as they are hungry after the long winter months of hibernation.

'As the day wore on, everyone was getting more worried by the minute.' Alex paused, stroking his forehead as though to prod his memory.

'My father found me. He always resorted to a glass of brandy when he was troubled. He made his way to his sanctuary, his office, to pour himself a drink to decide what to do next. On his way, he passed a second drawing room that was not in use; it had dust covers over the furniture. The door was usually locked, but something made him hesitate and try the door handle: unexpectedly, it was open.

'There I was, in the middle of the large room, standing in awe admiring the painting of a nude woman. I was mesmerised.'

Alex kept the stories coming: stories about people, events, and incidences percolating like a good coffee - capturing the essence of life.

When Peter and Camille started exchanging looks to indicate that they should be on their way, Alex cleverly steered the topic onto politics, arguing that perhaps CEOs deserved the outrageously high salaries and bonuses because of the dividends they provided to investors. Camille immediately reacted, even though she was aware that she was being teased, once again.

Peter, however, put a stop to the discussion. 'Come on, Camille, we have to get up for work tomorrow.'

On the drive back home, Peter chided his wife for yielding to Alex's tactics.

'I just think he enjoys baiting me and comes up with whatever he thinks will keep me hooked. You have to admit he still has an agile mind, the way he can steer his argument to support a point of view he does not really believe in!'

<><><>

Peter and Camille took it in turns to call Alex every day. Two week later, Camille was returning to her office after a tiresome meeting when her mobile phone rang.

'Hello Camille,' Alex said in a troubled voice. 'I'm having trouble finding my cheque book. I've looked everywhere. June is here.' June was his weekly cleaner, cum housekeeper. 'And I won't be able to pay her. I'm worried that with all the services that come in to help, it's gone missing.'

'Now hold on Alex,' Camille quickly put in. 'It's probably just misplaced. Whatever you do, don't phone and complain until we are sure it is truly missing...'

Once again Camille found herself driving north in the middle of the day.

Alex welcomed her in. June was about to leave.

'How much is owing?' Camille asked June, reaching for her purse.

'Oh, don't worry, dear,' June told her. 'I'll be back next week, and that'll do!'

When she left, Camille looked suspiciously at Alex. Then she asked, 'Who was the last person to visit before June?'

'Let's have a nice cup of tea first. The pot is brewing, ready.'

Camille held firm when Alex was about to embark on one of his stories. 'First we must locate the missing cheque book. So take me through yesterday. I think you said you had the gardener here?'

'Yes, of course,' Alex gave me a broad smile. 'I probably left it out in the shed – or in the office, where I keep the key to the shed. But shouldn't we have the sandwiches that June prepared for us before they go dry?'

'Sandwiches? Let's put our mind to rest first,' Camille insisted, her suspicions confirmed. Sure enough, there was his chequebook – in his key drawer. Camille looked hard at Alex. She knew he was playing up yet again. Camille felt that her dear friend had completed the circle of life and was returning to childhood duplicity when children want your attention at all costs.

Camille finished a delicious chicken and mustard sandwich and a second cup of tea - without whisky! Then she stood up and grabbed her bag, ready to leave.

'You know,' Alex started out, 'We seem to have lost our moral compass. It's all about the economy nowadays. Life has become a game of monopoly.'

Camille turned and looked closely at her dear friend. Alex wore a solemn expression, reflecting his concern of the state of affairs. She sat down again. 'What do you mean?' she asked.

<><><>

It was the broad grin on Alex's face that got

Camille back to earth, a full half hour later.

'Peter and I will see you in the weekend. But I must return to work!' She got up resolutely and, with a peck on his cheek, she took her leave.

As she drove away one more time, Camille broke into a smile. The wily old codger! He had done it again - roped her in to stay longer. Hooked, as it were!

...But then – as with lasting friendships – Camille knew that she had been hooked for a long time!

The End

A Special Request from the Author

Word-of-mouth is crucial for any author to succeed. If you enjoyed this collection of short stories, please consider leaving a review wherever you bought the book. Even if it is only a comment, it would make all the difference and would be very much appreciated.

Should you want to connect or learn more about the author you can do this at either FaceBook or Goodreads.

Facebook.com/ChristinaGillgrenAuthor

Goodreads.com - Christina Gillgren

Acknowledgements

The inspiration for this collection of short stories came about during a number of summers spent on the island of Malta.

Thanks to the great friends and the wonderful regulars who frequent Simenta - a beach concession in St Paul's Bay – I was able to familiarise myself once more with the rich fabric of life and tangled relations of my island of birth.

A small, densely populated island where everyone seems to know everybody else - or about them - lends itself to fertile chatter and intrigue. It was a natural place to give birth to the ideas for this collection of short stories. Whilst some of the characters in the book are inspired by colourful individuals and many humorous events and goings-on, the stories are a work of fiction, products of the author's imagination let loose - except where noted otherwise with (*).

Once again, I am lucky enough to have been surrounded by wonderful people who have helped in so many ways.

I would like to thank my sister Josianne for

keeping me going with my writing, and for her encouragement and enthusiasm, helping with 'twists' as she road-tested some of the story plots.

This book would never have found its way to publication were it not for the tremendous hard work, help and patience of my husband and partner, Bjorn. He is also my first editor, publisher and collaborator. Special thanks are also due to Bjorn's brother Dan for helping with technological issues.

I must give credit to "Unsplash" that provides beautiful, free images gifted by the world's most generous community of photographers. The cover of this book is clear evidence of the quality of material to be found there.

I would also like to give special thanks to my editor, Teresa Culbert, for painstakingly going through the manuscript and for her invaluable feedback. However, I absolve her of all responsibility for my linguistic quirks.

As always, love and thanks to my wonderful family for their encouragement and support: Mark and Bridget, and Annika and AJ. You have enriched our lives in so many ways.

A Tease Read:

About A Little Bit of MisChief

"We had a dream ...a dream that one day we would set off into the sunset. And then circumstances beyond our control threw up a dilemma and we decided to take the plunge: quit work and set off to make it a journey without leaving footprints, only smiles."

A Little Bit of MisChief is a light hearted, whimsical account of the author and her husband's seven year adventure sailing from Australia to the Mediterranean and beyond. This is a journey sprinkled with exhilarating experiences that include sandstorms at sea and tropical water spouts, heart pounding moments with pirates, swimming with whale sharks and dolphins in some of the most exotic waters, amazingly generous characters and of course lasting friendships and laughter along the way.

It is a story about what fulfilling a dream might bring if you persist and take the plunge.

Reviews for A Little Bit of MisChief

'The author's adventures are told so vividly, making it so blissfully and effortlessly easy to picture being there, or just following her paths to perhaps make up your very own 'bucket-list' of the must-see, sublime spots mentioned in her book.'

Nadine Muscat Cini, *Freelance Lifestyle Journalist, Times of Malta*

'*A Little Bit of MisChief* is a great read full of memories of an unforgettable trip. Most of all it depicts how anyone can take the challenge and make the dream their own.'

Phil Ross, *Australian Cruising Helmsman*

'Christina's tales of heart pounding moments with pirates and swimming with whale sharks and dolphins in exotic waters, among many others. Christina's story is a tribute to the perilous journey many brave Maltese men and women undertook, often also by boat, in search of a better life and to follow their dreams. Christina's own adventure almost 'a migrants journey in reverse'

Marie Benoît, *The Malta Independent*

'..a delightful cruising book... May many 'dreamers' enjoy Christina's book and perhaps go cruising in such an enjoyable way...'

Peter Campbell, *AFLOAT*

Reader reviews

'Great book, Great writer, loved her book. A Little Bit of Mischief is a good read, funny and interesting.' - Sharon Verry'

'I loved the book from the first page. Couldn't put it down. It was like being there, sharing the adventure.' - Nallen Karlsson

'Loved this book, learnt way more than I ever knew about boating !! It took me on such a ride I was wishing I could go too....it has opened up a whole new world for me.' - Karyl

'This is great read - an inspirational story of travel and a true partnership.' - Cec Broderick

'One of my favorite Christmas presents was

A tease read: A Little Bit of MisChief

"A Little Bit of Mischief" Looking forward to reading the next one.' - Nancy V. Jaderen

'Golly it's great. I cannot get my nose out of it.' - Lynne Newton

'I thoroughly enjoyed it... what an amazing journey...' - Clare Crusham

'The description is so natural I feel as though I'm living the moments.' - Josephine Gatt

'What an excellent read.' - Helen Corbett

1

Launching a Dream

It all started one Australian summer evening when Bjorn, my husband, was surfing the net. Here we were, both in our early to mid-fifties, bogged down with work, long hours, high stress jobs and mobile phones constantly ringing: Bjorn even had two work phones, one of which we referred to as the 'death' phone, which was when he would receive notification of fatalities in a work place. Being in charge of occupational health and safety in Western Australia, where we lived, was no joke and we often wondered about the toll the working hours were taking on our health.

It did not help that I worked for the State Premier running a small Office as a public policy advisor. I was entrusted with the task of empowering citizen participation and making public policy decisions more inclusive and accountable. We valued living in beautiful, sunny Perth, Western Australia, the land of the sandgropers with their love of the outdoors. Sandgropers, incidentally, are tough, resolute insects closely related to grasshoppers and locusts. This moniker is the colloquial name for Western Australians and their laid-back but tenacious approach to life. Yet here we were, stressed out and running around with mobile phones to our ears. So where did we go wrong? Surely there was an alternative to this madness.

"Wouldn't it be lovely to leave all this behind?"

"Yes, but can we afford it ...and what would we do instead?"

Discussions on a lifestyle change had become a frequent evening topic, as we sat on our balcony with a glass of vino in hand, chilling out after a long day: the dreaming, we used to call it! Our sanity was called *Salina*. She was a Sparkman and Stevens (S&S) 40-foot sailing boat, just right for the stiff sea breezes that blow, often at 25 knots and more (Force Six), along the Perth coast all spring and summer. No boat, either before or after, has ever come near the way our *Salina* cut through the water. Much as we loved her, though, we knew she was not our choice for long term cruising. She was built along more traditional lines with a narrow stern and little storage space. *Salina* was a gorgeous boat to sail and race in, but if we were going to make it our home for a few years at least, there was not much room for comfort.

Our dreaming involved conjuring up the ideal boat, with a variety of names from *Water Music* to *Anchor Song* and finally to *Salina 2*. The boat Bjorn saw listed on the internet was a Moody, a 43-foot sailing boat built in Britain for serious ocean cruising. And very comfortable with lots of room for the long-term cruiser.

"Come look at this, Chris."

In our frequent discussions on what we would do and where we would go, we had narrowed down the type of boat that suited our purpose to a couple of brands. A 'Moody' was close to the top of our list. She also had the one prerequisite from my point of view: a lovely detached queen size, centre line bed accessible from both sides, with loads of headroom. Not for us the squashed berths where you have to climb over each other, with hardly any room for a good bonk! We had a healthy love life and we certainly wanted to keep it that way.

What made her even more attractive was the fact that this particular boat was fully equipped for going round the world. She was a sturdy boat, tried and tested. The Swiss owner had sailed her from Spain across the Atlantic and the Pacific Oceans. But then he got impatient waiting for good weather in Tonga. The result was a horrible crossing to New Zealand when he ran into a terrible storm. That was the end of sailing for him. For us, the boat was conveniently located in the Bay of Islands, tied up from freedom, awaiting a new owner and some more adventure.

It was just by chance that the following week I was scheduled to fly from Perth to Canberra for work. Luckily, Bjorn was flying to Sydney on another work-related trip at the same time. Auckland, New Zealand, was a stone's throw away for us both, and from there we proceeded to Opua in the Bay of Islands.

Talk about love at first sight! She was a typical Moody. As she swayed jauntily along the pier, I could already picture her and her playful 'mood' and the name just came to me: *Mischief*, spirited and free, and ready to sail off and sprinkle our path with fun and adventure. She was just the right size, one I was able to handle singlehanded if necessary. I wanted a touch of cheek, laughter and friendships to be the hallmark of our future - and a smile to be the first response of those who crossed paths with us.

Due to Australian importation and tax laws, it became more feasible to purchase the boat in Australia. Our helpful boat broker arranged for the boat to be sailed across the Tasman Sea to Brisbane, where ownership would be transferred to us. And so *Mischief* began her new life.

Jomaro, as the boat was then called, was in a 'tired' state when we flew out to welcome her in Brisbane. I had negotiated with Julie, a veteran sailor who was to become a good friend, to sail her to Fremantle, the seaport to Perth. Here we would work on her and prepare her for her new cruising life. With an all women crew, Julie sailed the boat from Brisbane to Fremantle over the top of Australia, a trip of almost 4000 nautical miles. A few glitches along the way reflected once again the sorry state that *Jomaro* had fallen into. I flew to Darwin in August, getting away from mid-winter in Perth, to help sail her down the Western Australian coast.

"This is exciting! I'm so looking forward to this trip, but I confess to being a bit uneasy. I really do not like crocodiles." I had heard so much about the vast, untamed northern coast of Western Australia with crocodile infested waters, king tides that can reach up to 11 metres and above, and a wild desolate coastline with little habitation.

Julie soon put an end to my speculation, however. "We'll be sailing in two to four day hops," she told me. "This way we will get to Perth faster, and won't have much problem with the tides, as we will be well away from the coast. Hopefully, it will be a smooth run."

On our first day at sea, a coast guard planc approached and swept down to fly past our stern. Soon they were calling us on the radio.

"Sailing vessel with white hull and blue canvas. This is the Australian Coast Guard. Please identify yourself."

"Australian Coast Guard. This is sailing yacht *Jomaro*: Juliet, Oscar, Mike, Alpha, Romeo, Oscar...."

"Sailing yacht *Jomaro*: Last port of call and

destination, please?"

"Last port of call was Darwin, we left one day ago. We are making our way south having come round all the way from Brisbane. Our next port of call will be Dampier."

"OK, *Jomaro*. Have a good trip."

...And they came back the second day, and the third.... Suddenly the world had grown smaller. The feeling of isolation dissolved. There was no way we could be lost here.

On our second day at sea, a large pod of whales caught up with us off the coast at Wyndham.

"Hey, guys. Look at that!" I marvelled, awed by the sheer number of whales, spouting water, breaching and turning the sea into a maelstrom of froth. "There must be close to a hundred."

Julie immediately got up, looking anxiously around, and I soon realised why.

"Shit, what the hell is that!" I shouted, startled and worried at the same time. I was at the helm keeping a lookout, and a whale had breached right next to us, so close that I could almost reach out and touch its enormous tail.

"That looks like a calf." Julie warned. "Make

sure you don't get between her and her mum!"

"And how am I going to do that?" I muttered to myself. The whales had overtaken us and all we could do was hold our breath and hope for the best. Luckily, they swam past and moved on without incident, though not without a spectacular splash or two to show who the masters of this marine universe were.

We had terrific weather with just the right amount of wind to propel us south. The rest of the trip was uneventful. We spent some lovely mornings getting to know each other, appreciating the serenity of the boat cutting through the water. We chatted away happily on everything from sailing and cruising to politics. Julie was an excellent skipper, always unruffled and yet, ever watchful and ready; she was an excellent role model.

One evening, as sunset approached, Julie introduced me to the 'green flash' phenomenon.

"Watch the sunset, as the sun hits the water," she started out. And sure enough, as the sun ducked into the horizon, a brief tinge of green appeared on its upper rim.

"What causes that?"

"Not sure..."

"Perhaps it's the combination of the blue water with the yellow sun?" I wondered. I found out later that this was a visual wonder that came about in certain conditions.

Another amazing sight was the 'cat eyes'. As the moon set one evening, a pair of cat eyes stood out on the horizon. Again, Julie pointed them out to me.

"That's really strange; almost unsettling," I started out. The twin tips of what was left visible of the setting moon shone eerily over the horizon. This only happens when the waxing or waning moon crescent is lying horizontal.

We enjoyed a stopover in Broome where we had to tackle the tides for the first time. Julie set the anchor a good distance from the shore, ensuring we would still have enough depth as the tide receded. We took the rubber dinghy ashore, laden with diesel cans and shopping bags, to be greeted by an old friend who lived in the town. It was great to be able to stretch our legs and walk about after almost two weeks on board.

"Hey, what happened to the water?" I said as

we returned to the beach, much to the amusement of Julie and Margaret. Our dinghy lay stranded a good 50 metres from the water's edge.

"Now you see why I wanted to consult the tide tables." Julie smiled at me, as we vainly tried to drag the dinghy with outboard motor on the stern - and four jerry cans full of diesel - down the now exposed beach.

Not one to give up easily, I took hold of the bow, turned the dinghy around so that the stern was towards the water, lifted and pushed, and let the large wheels on the back of the dinghy do their work.

"*Voila*!" I said triumphantly. But I had also learnt my lesson: never mess with the tidcs.

It was with great sadness that I waved goodbye to Julie and Margaret at Carnarvon, our next stop. Three weeks had flown past, and I had to return to work. The trip had strengthened my resolve to set off and sail the boat westward. *Jomaro* was a sound and steady boat, ideal for cruising. She behaved well with a following sea. Even the two to three day passages keeping watch night and day had not put me off. Rather, they simply confirmed that sailing was indeed the right antidote to our current mad life.

It took a turn of events at my workplace to push us past the dream stage. Following a change of State Premier, my office underwent a series of transformations, with the new leadership looking to change our focus. There was no love or enthusiasm for the work my office was doing, and I had had enough of the political spin. It was time for a change. I was well positioned to branch off as a consultant, and did so to start with. However, the zest and interest were lacking. I craved the freedom to embrace a life of adventure. It was in this context that the plan to set off sailing in about four to six years' time got thrown out of the window, together with caution to the wind. A formal departure date was set for Easter 2008, six months hence.

Our initial thoughts were to sail to Southeast Asia, and get our sea legs before setting out to cross the Indian Ocean. We then hoped to sail up the Red Sea to the Mediterranean, and finally to the island of Malta. This is where I originated from before coming to settle in Perth with my Swedish-born husband, Bjorn, some 35 years ago. We estimated our journey back to Europe would take a couple of years and then we would see how things evolved.

Six hectic months followed in which *Jomaro* was stripped, and every bolt and rivet checked. With Julie's help, the interior was sanded and varnished. I spent a great deal of time chasing 'tradies' to do the work, and I can also now confirm that WA stands for 'Wait Awhile', as some of the trades gave us the run around.

Work involved replacing the 'crazed' acrylic glass and rubber seals in all the portholes and hatches to ensure they were watertight. With Bjorn's help, we removed the ceiling in the main cabin, which was stained yellow with cigarette smoke and re-sprayed it. To complement the renovation, I ordered new upholstery foam and covers throughout. I even had a queen size mattress made up. These were complemented with fresh fitted carpets and curtains. Meanwhile Bjorn took the galley apart, installed a new fridge/freezer. A shipwright helped rebuild the galley, to replace the worn timber and surfaces.

Within a couple of months, *Jomaro* was transformed. Soon it was a case of putting it all together again in readiness for a new life. Bjorn went through the electrics changing most of the wiring to the tinned copper wiring type that better withstands the salt-water environment. Then he turned his attention to all things mechanical, including the wind generator. And finally, we checked all the sails and ordered a new storm jib. Luckily for us, the rigging and the instrumentation were fairly new, as *Jomaro* had been struck by lightning in the Caribbean and everything had been changed as a result.

One of the wonders of owning a Bluewater, ocean-going cruiser is that life can be so self-sufficient. We could generate our own power with the aid of the wind and the sun, and make our own fresh water with our inboard water maker. We were eager to test them out to see how they would serve us once we were out and about, away from civilization.

Of course, being sailors, the boat underwent a de-naming ceremony: champagne, and a solemn thanking of the boat for having carried all aboard safely during its life as *Jomaro*. A week later, as is customary in boating circles, the newly refurbished *Mischief* was christened in a lovely welcoming ceremony and yet another bottle of champers. Not to put too fine a point to it, I performed the ceremony - amidst a host of friends, sailors and landlubbers - with great gusto: a swig for me, and a swig for the bow; another swig for me and one for the stern; and so it went on, for port and then for starboard, with my swigs in-between. I was soon swaying about merrily, even though we were still on dry land.

After this thorough drenching to ensure she was appropriately launched, we had a moment of solemnity as I beseeched *Mischief* to deliver us with 'fair winds and following seas' to exotic places in safety. It proved to be a very cheerful occasion as the champagne flowed freely and our guests matched each of my swigs, charging their glasses to toast our new boat.

Watching the goings-on, my daughter quipped, "Yes... hmm... 'Miss Chief' at it again, I see!"

There was sadness at leaving our daughter Annika, her partner and Chika, that beautiful half-human dog of hers. But her encouragement and enthusiasm drove us on.

"I'm so proud of you," she told us. "We'll definitely come and join you somewhere!"

Our son Mark and his wife were living in London at this stage. Being globetrotters and adventure lovers, they were thrilled about our plans, and did not hold back in encouraging us to follow our dreams and make them reality.

"Send us your itinerary," Mark told us. "We'll join you wherever we can."

A couple of weeks later we faced the challenge of moving from a large house onto a boat. Whilst we did not sell our home, which we intended to lease out to fund our trip, we had to deal with the contents accumulated over a lifetime. With packing up house, arranging to auction off most of our furniture, and organising our affairs whilst overseas, we were soon running around ragged.

I couldn't help but compare dealing with our worldly goods with winding up the estate of dear adopted grandparents of ours two years previously. It seemed weird that we were now doing the same with our possessions: "this stays, this is for auction, this goes into storage ...and this is for the bin!" Except, of course, that we were still well and truly alive.

Hectic though it was I felt charged with energy. This was a pivotal moment in our sea change.

Bjorn and I moved on board just before Christmas 2007 to start our lives as live-a-boards. It was an awesome moment. *Mischief* was now our home, and we found her welcoming and cosy. We did not neglect the comfort items. We purchased a flat screen television and DVD player. At one of the boating and camping shops, we acquired a wonderfully compact washing machine, the envy of many sailors. Even more useful was the gas barbecue that Bjorn set up on the pushpit, the railing on the back of a boat, for all the fish we intended to catch and feast on all the way to the Mediterranean. This was apart from the stereo system with indoor and outdoor speakers. To power it all there was a large battery set, with battery to mains power converters for kitchen gadgets.

At this stage, Bjorn had not yet sailed the boat once. Something had to be done about this. Therefore, on Boxing Day, we set off with fellow sailors from the Fremantle Sailing Club on the two-week shakedown cruise to Quindalup, south of Perth. This was a good opportunity to check everything out, commission the water maker and generally ensure that the boat was self-contained enough to keep us going between ports.

We spoke to as many long-term sailors as we could find but they were thin on the ground in Fremantle. The few who had made it round the world, like Jim and Margaret, were very supportive. My friend Julie, a long-time sailor, helped organise ship's stores and sea charts. For the booze, I have to confess to being an aficionado of long standing, though in moderate quantities and always in company. They say 'shared sorrow is sorrow halved and that shared happiness is happiness doubled'. May I also add that with a bottle of good red this works even better.

Our first destinations in Asia were predominantly 'dry' countries, and so we stocked the boat bilges with eight dozen bottles of red and white wine plus about another 50 litres of cask wine. The boat was bursting at its seams with an endless supply of canned tuna, pasta, rice, sauces, and a variety of canned fruit. This was in addition to the 400 litres of water and 460 litres of diesel we carried. No wonder the waterline on *Mischief* sank by about 10 centimetres.

It's funny how we would go out sailing in practically all weather and never worry about anything when based in Fremantle. Then suddenly we were leaving on this big cruise and the nerves kicked in.

One of our wisest decisions was the plan to have Admiral Julie, as we now called her, accompany us for the first couple of weeks, sitting quietly in the background enjoying the sail, exuding calm. This turned out to be a prudent choice, especially as Bjorn had yet to learn so many of *Mischief's* quirks.

Julie introduced us to cruising guides, covering almost all sailed parts of the world. These guides are similar to the *Lonely Planet* type of guides for land travellers, but contain valuable information for sailors: weather, local customs, visas, permits, port entry requirements, and of course safe anchorages and harbours. The *Western Australian Cruising Guide* enabled us to draw up a rough plan for our passage up along the west coast of Australia. Cruising guides also provide details of facilities available at different destinations, such as laundries and types of shops available. In addition, Jimmy Cornell's *World Cruising*

Routes offered essential advice on the best passages between locations, and especially across oceans. All were necessary, as our knowledge of passages at this stage was pretty close to abysmal.

We set the departure date for 24 April 2008, heading north to the Abrolhos Islands outside Geraldton for around 10 days before continuing up the Western Australian coast. Our club, the Fremantle Sailing Club, organises a cruise up the Western Australian coast to the Abrolhos Islands every year. This seemed a good spring broad to start our passage north. From there we would take off on our own and continue up the coast as far as Broome. We would check out of Australia at this location and head to Indonesia, probably to Kupang or to Bali. The plan was to spend six months in south-east Asia, gently making our way northwards to arrive in Thailand by the end of the year, as this was the best time for crossing the Indian Ocean in a westerly direction. We expected to be able to visit Sri Lanka, the Maldives, and the Seychelles along the way, before going up the Red Sea to the Suez Canal. This would bring us to the Mediterranean around April or May 2009.

As the start of our cruising adventure loomed closer, Bjorn and I were run off our feet with last minute checks: not a bad thing, given the cocktail of excitement and nerves. It didn't help when my wrist played up. After months of sanding and varnishing, I had aggravated an old condition and now needed surgery for carpal tunnel syndrome. I hoped this would only leave me out of action for a couple of weeks, during which time I could concentrate on the passage preparation and stocking the boat.

With many countries now asking for sailing qualifications, Bjorn and I turned to the paperwork. Bjorn was a certified ship's master from his days in the Marines in Sweden. He was registered to handle boats up to 300 tons (*Mischief* was twelve tons). Meanwhile, I immediately signed up with Yachting Australia for an Offshore Yacht Master's course, to complement the Coastal Skipper's certification I already held.

Next on our list were the radios on board: *Mischief* was equipped with a short wave radio for talking to other boats, marinas, and any ports or harbours we approached; there was also, more importantly, a HF Single Side Band

(SSB) long-range radio for when we were out in the middle of nowhere. With this, we could always access weather forecasts, so vital especially when traversing an ocean.

"We need a licence to operate this," Bjorn informed me, referring to the SSB radio. And so, we enrolled in the appropriate course at our sailing club and got our licences. The next step was to register the HF radio with the authorities in Australia and we were allocated our call sign: WAN3065 (Whiskey [appropriate, given my love of this golden liquid], Alpha, November 3065) which would identify us in case of emergencies.

"I'm a free man," Bjorn hugged me as he returned home from work for the final time after having handed in his resignation a month previously. It was the 28th March, and not a moment too soon for Bjorn to get used to being on the boat 24/7. Slowly things started falling into place. After three months on the leasing market, our house looked set to go as we signed up some good tenants for a couple of years. This would be our main source of income during our travels, leaving all our savings intact.

The reality of this incredible sea change was gradually sinking in. At this point, we were in an almost trance-like state and did everything on automatic pilot. As our sailing friends realised we were serious about sailing away into the horizon they became very supportive: we ended up with three doctors offering to advise us on a comprehensive first aid kit for sailors. I will always remember with fondness a lovely neighbour of ours, a renowned surgeon, showing us how to do sutures using a raw chicken breast to practice on.

Our land-based friends were just as caring and helpful, although somewhat concerned. We were touched at how they ensured we would be kept in mind whilst we were away on our escapade. Our bi-monthly dinner group consisted of five couples, all of whom - except for us - were great Footy (Australian Rules football) fans. They had a medal cast that they called the "Gillgren Medal" in our honour. This was awarded at the end of each season to the person who scored the highest in the footy tipping.

We had done our best to ensure we prepared as well as we could: *Mischief* was a serious blue water cruiser and could handle tough conditions. We needed to ensure that we were also up to the task as best we could. And then as D-Day drew close, so did the panic, with scribbled lists and last minute suggestions.

"How about a first-aid course" Bjorn proposed.

"And a 'survival-at-sea' training course would also help," I added.

We were lucky to be able to enrol for these courses at the last minute. Boat and dinghy engines were serviced with the help of professionals. Bjorn went through as much equipment as he could; for example checking the inflation cylinders to the life jackets. Flares were updated, a new emergency EPIRB (Emergency Position Indicating Radio Beacon) was installed and registered with the appropriate maritime authorities, and life jackets examined and tested. We took the life raft in for an inflation test and had it re-equipped with emergency rations. It was then down to the last shopping spree, loading the boat with as much fresh food as we thought would survive.

However much you achieve, you still end up with this long list. But we felt we had the basics right and the time had come for our departure.

The panic was gone. In its stead there was elation, excitement and anticipation. We were practically chafing at the bit to take off on our adventure.

We motored out of Fremantle harbour on the 24th April 2008. We proudly set the Australian flag on the boat's stern and the Fremantle Sailing Club burgee on the spreaders. It was a sunny day with light, variable winds. Friends lined the breakwater, waving us off as we set sail to Andrea Bocelli's 'Time to say Goodbye'. Accompanying us to help us, especially Bjorn, adjust to the boat's quirks were Julie and her friend Margaret.

"Now, where's that sunset!" Bjorn quipped. To which I responded "Hey-Ho! And away we go. This calls for a drink!"

We popped open the first bottle of champagne at sea. Mind you, this broke our agreed rule of no drink while under way. But then, rules are made to be broken, aren't they?

A tease read: A Little Bit of MisChief

Boat Christening

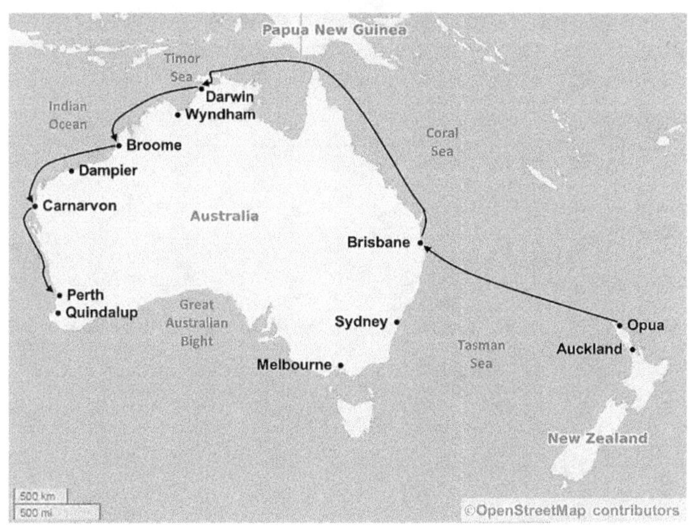

Boat Delivery Route: Opua to Fremantle

2

A Fishy Start

After the hectic running around to get ready for departure, it was heaven to sit on the boat and watch the world go by.

We were lucky in that the forecast north-easterly winds were delivered in gentle doses, enabling us to motor-sail up the coast. It was a case of testing the engine out, as we made our way to Mindarie in the Perth northern suburbs - and onto our first minor mishap as we tried to tie up to the jetty in Mindarie Marina. A slight miscalculation with a strong current pushed the boat onto the quay, which resulted in our losing the port navigation light.

“Dammit! Is it a write-off?”

“’fraid so. We’ll have to replace it. Hope we can get a matching one, as this one looks like it was part of the original boat.” We had sensibly taken a chandlery catalogue with us, so we could identify any boat parts we would require and order them wherever we found ourselves. A quick check and Bjorn told me “I think we are in luck. This looks similar to what we have.”

We had officially left Fremantle, but we had not left Perth. Our children plus in-laws joined us for a final farewell dinner, more hugs and kisses. Then we spent a restful night at the quay without further mishap.

The next morning, the promised easterly winds arrived. We left the marina nice and early for our first overnight trip to Port Dennison. Averaging a decent five to six knots in the light to moderate wind, we headed out to sea, but our relaxation was short lived. Before long, we found ourselves winding our way through a nightmare of cray pots. Avoiding them in the daylight was not too problematic, but what were we going to do if one of them got tangled around our propeller during the night?

To make matters worse, at around 4.00am

the wind veered to the north-east which was right on the nose. Trying unsuccessfully to get some sleep down below, I heard Bjorn mutter as we brushed against yet another craypot in the increasingly bumpy seas. Not a good first night out.

It was not long before the wind blew up to around 22 knots. The waves built up, making the ride uncomfortable. We continued tacking northwards, but then we had to turn on the motor for the last five miles to reach the shelter of Port Dennison and get out of the swell.

We spent a few days waiting for better weather, checking everything out, glad that all seemed to be working well. We passed the time swimming and exploring the surrounds. Admiral Julie introduced us to fish trawling: driving around in the dinghy at low speed with a line out the back. But we had no luck.

Our next stop was Geraldton, and we had a pleasant day at sea, sailing into the harbour in the afternoon. We called in at the fuel jetty to do some shopping for fresh goods. Then we motored around to the north of the harbour to anchor overnight in preparation for a very early morning start to our trip across to the Abrolhos islands, a small archipelago west of Geraldton.

We had to leave at 2.00am to get to the archipelago at midday, which is always the best time to approach reefs. It was a bumpy night with thunderstorms and squalls, but as morning rolled on the weather calmed down and the sun came out in all its glory. This was a bonus as, with the sun directly overhead, you can see the reefs more clearly and navigate through them safely.

As we approached the atolls, we were confronted with a fascinating, magical sight: a line of low-level buildings, which ....

www.ingramcontent.com/pod-product-compliance
Lightning Source LLC
Chambersburg PA
CBHW070117120726
47909CB00002B/637

* 9 7 8 0 6 4 8 5 4 2 9 2 6 *